Tamed for the Lion

A NOVEL BY

Annabelle Winters

Books by Annabelle Winters

The CURVES FOR SHEIKHS Series

Curves for the Sheikh
Flames for the Sheikh
Hostage for the Sheikh
Single for the Sheikh
Stockings for the Sheikh
Untouched for the Sheikh
Surrogate for the Sheikh
Stars for the Sheikh
Shelter for the Sheikh
Shared for the Sheikh
Assassin for the Sheikh
Privilege for the Sheikh
Ransomed for the Sheikh
Uncorked for the Sheikh
Haunted for the Sheikh
Grateful for the Sheikh
Mistletoe for the Sheikh
Fake for the Sheikh

The CURVES FOR SHIFTERS Series

Curves for the Dragon
Born for the Bear
Witch for the Wolf
Tamed for the Lion
Taken for the Tiger

TAMED FOR THE LION

A NOVEL BY

ANNABELLE WINTERS

2019
RAINSHINE BOOKS
USA

Copyright Notice

TAMED FOR THE LION

PROLOGUE
<u>ADAM'S LAIR</u>
<u>THE CASPIAN SEA</u>

"**F**inding Darius the Lion isn't gonna be that hard," said Caleb the Wolf, staring at the massive computer screen projected up on the wall of Adam's study in the bowels of the white castle. "There aren't that many circuses these days—especially circuses with performing animals."

"There shouldn't be *any* circuses with animals in them," said Bis the Leopard Shifter. She folded her arms beneath her breasts as her mate Bart the Bear glanced down shamelessly at her chest and grinned. "We aren't performing monkeys, you know."

"That's disrespectful to monkeys, babe," said Bart the Bear, his grin widening as he casually placed his big paw on Bis's large ass.

"Stop monkeying around, you two," scolded Ash, Bart's younger sister, a bear Shifter herself. "Caleb's right. We haven't thought this through. If we want to help Shifters get together with their mates, we need to figure out how to find *both* mates."

"Sounds like that's a problem for the girls in this crew," said Bart with a grunt. "We find the guy. You chicks find the girl."

Adam the Alpha Dragon smiled at the smug, overgrown bear. "I should remind you that *you* haven't done shit yet besides defend the rights of monkeys to not be insulted. What is it with you and the great apes, anyway? All that time in the South American rainforest hanging with the monkeys, I suppose. Did you tell them you were an ape like them? Or did they just assume you were because of the funny faces you make when you break things?"

"Can we show some respect for our ape brethren, please?" said Bart, placing his sledgehammer-sized fists on his hips and sticking out his chest. He glanced at Caleb. "I'm pretty sure there were a couple of silverback gorilla Shifters in Murad's army. Those apes don't monkey around."

"Here we go," said Caleb, his voice low, a seriousness breaking through the playful atmosphere in the room. He leaned back on his chair as he zoomed in on an image from the Internet. "Here he is. Darius the Lion Shifter. Anyone feel like this is still a joke?"

The room went silent as all six Shifters stared up at the screen. On it was a bare-chested man with a thick mane of deep-gold hair, sand-colored eyes that were looking directly into the camera, thick red lips twisted into a casual sneer of pure superiority. His arms were stretched out wide, his massive, tanned pectorals looking like slabs of bronze armor, the contours of his ab muscles casting shadows on his body. In his right hand was a whip made of old leather, its ends frayed and battered like it had been used to its full capabilities.

"When was this taken?" said Magda the Witch,

a fox Shifter who was Caleb's fated mate—and the mother of seven pups. She narrowed her eyes as she went close to the screen. "And where?"

Caleb zoomed in on the image's caption. "Three days ago. Istanbul, Turkey. But the circus has moved on. They're probably on the road now. The next stop is Morocco."

"Northern Africa?" said Adam with a frown. He leaned over Caleb's shoulder and punched a few keys, bringing up the circus's schedule. "That's interesting. They've got a lot of dates scheduled all over Africa. Very puzzling."

"Why is it puzzling? Don't Africans like circuses?" said Ash.

Adam smiled at his mate, but his expression betrayed his racing mind. "I'm sure they like circuses just fine. But so do the Europeans, who have much more money to spend. Why would the circus travel all the way from Turkey down to Africa without making some money in Europe along the way? It doesn't make sense."

"Unless Darius is running the show now," said Caleb softly, flipping back to a picture of the lion shifter with his circus animals. It was a magnificent photograph, in vivid color, with Darius bare-chested in the center of the ring, surrounded by fourteen massive lions, all of them staring at him with their gold eyes like they were in a trance. He was clearly in control of those animals, and Caleb grunted as he leaned back in his chair. "Lions aren't like dragons. They don't care about money so much. What they crave is . . . power. Power, dominion, ownership and obedience," he said slowly, rubbing his buzzed head and grunting again. "It just occurred to me: Almost all the world's lion population is found in the jungles of Africa, isn't that right?"

Bis the Leopard nodded. "Tigers are found in Asia. Lions in Africa. There are some lions in India, but you're right—most of the world's lions are in the African continent. What of it?"

"I don't know," Caleb said. "But there's a connection. Darius is planning something. And if he's still under Murad's control, it's probably not good."

Bart stepped forward, his meaty paw slamming against the keyboard and making the screen go blank. "Here's a suggestion, boys. Instead of sitting here drinking tea and staring at a half-naked dude on a computer screen, how about we just get our asses to Africa and straight-up *ask* this big pussycat what he's got planned! Any of you geniuses thought of that?"

Caleb grinned as he looked up at Bart the Bear. "Have you ever tried to interrogate a Lion Shifter, Butterball?"

"Well, no," said Bart with a shrug. "But how hard can it be? I hold him upside down by his ankles, and you punch him in the face until he tells us everything!"

Everyone laughed except Magda the Witch, who had stepped back from the group and was muttering something under her breath. Suddenly her face went blank, a thick vein on her forehead pulsing as her eyes rolled up in her head.

"Magda!" Caleb said, leaping up from his chair and rushing over to his mate. "What's happening? What do you see?"

Magda let out a slow, trembling breath, her eyelids fluttering as she muttered those silent words under her breath. Finally she blinked herself back to reality, glancing around the room like she'd lost track of where she was.

"Two women," she said, her lips tightening into a strange smile as if she was only just realizing what she'd seen. "I saw them like they were in the room. Two women. Two Shifters. One of them is Darius's mate. I can sense it."

"Give us more!" Ash said excitedly, stepping forward but keeping her distance from the witch, who'd been learning to balance her natural magic with dark magic that came through her sly, trickster fox. "Names. Descriptions. Locations. Anything we can use to track them down!"

Magda was silent, her eyes still rolled up in her head like she was having a mild seizure. She raised her hand as if to say, "Hold on. I'm trying!" and finally Bis spoke up, her voice soft but firm.

"If Darius does have a fated mate, then the universe will bring them together," said Bis, reaching for Bart's big arm. "That's what happened with all of us, wasn't it?"

"Yes," said Caleb, still staring at his mate Magda with some concern. "But we don't know what Darius's state of mind is right now. We don't know what his animal's state of mind is. Darius the Lion, Everett the Tiger . . . they were both under Murad's control, under the control of the Black Dragon, under the control of the Darkness that lives in every Shifter's animal. Their mission is to kill Shifters, not mate with them."

"Caleb's right," said Ash. "We might have to

help the universe on this one. Fate is going to have to operate through us. We can't just sit back and wait."

Suddenly Magda was back, her curvy natural body hunching over as she took a heaving breath like she'd been holding it all this while. Caleb grabbed on to her as she staggered from the effort of trying to probe her vision for more details, and when she regained her senses, she looked around the room and sighed.

"No, we can't just wait," she said. She looked into the eyes of each of the other two women in the room. "It was different for us. For all three of us women, our animals were dormant, buried, in hiding. Once they woke up—once *we* woke up— the universe guided us to our mates. But for these two women it's different."

"Different from us? How?" said Bis.

"Different in that their animals are alive and awake," said Magda, a tight smile emerging on her face. "These women already *know* that they're Shifters!"

"So shouldn't their animals be feeling drawn to their fated mates, pulled towards their destiny, just like we were?" said Ash.

"You would think. But it's not happening with

these women. There's something stopping them from following their paths," said Magda, her smile turning to a frown. "I sensed a deep bond between the two of them—a bond built on heartache, pain, upheaval. These are strong, determined, powerful women who at some point decided they didn't need a man, didn't need a mate, were just fine on their own."

Adam frowned as he slowly paced the room. "So these women know each other?"

"Yes," said Magda. "They're family. Sisters."

"And you know how to find them?" said Adam.

"I think so. Yes," said Magda.

"Great," said Bart, grinning as he glanced at Adam. "When do we leave?"

Magda shook her head. "It's not that simple. We can't just show up on their doorstep and tell them hey, one of you is Darius's mate. We have to let nature take its course. Put them in the same room as Darius somehow. Let their animals feel that primal pull towards each other. Throwing ourselves into the mix too early might just create chaos. Darius's Lion might try to kill us if we're in the area."

"Well, it might try to kill those two women too," said Bart, his square jaw tightening. "Putting them in the room with a Lion Shifter is like leading lambs to the slaughter."

"Except they aren't lambs," said Magda quietly, her eyes shining dark for a moment as if she was revisiting the image of the two sisters. "They're bobcats. Strong, stubborn, and relentless. Viciously protective of each other. Together they can hold their own against any Shifter."

Ash took a slow breath as she began to pace the room, her bare feet making no sound on the white stone floors. "But if these sisters are so close, connecting one of them with her mate might bring on another kind of resistance, another kind of chaos."

"Not if we manage to connect both of them with their mates," said Magda, glancing up at Caleb the Wolf. "There were two big cats in Murad's army, weren't there?"

Caleb nodded, his deep blue eyes narrowing. "Darius the Lion. Everett the Tiger. You think . . ."

"Yes, I do think that," said Magda, finally relaxing into a smile. "We start with the lion, and the Tiger will drop into place."

"A lion and a tiger," said Bis with a smile. "Mated with two bobcat sisters. Sounds like we've got a big-cat duet in the works, gang!"

"Meeee-owww!" roared Bart the Bear in the

highest pitch he could muster. Everyone laughed as the tension was broken momentarily. But the moment didn't last, because the big screen flickered back to life, that image of Darius surrounded by fourteen lions casting the dark room in a golden glow.

"So how do we do this?" said Bis softly, blinking at the screen and then looking away. "How do we get the bobcat sisters in the same room as Darius the Lion without things getting out of hand? After all, the Black Dragon's army has been tasked with *killing* Shifters, right?"

"Well," said Caleb, rubbing his tight jaw as he glanced at Magda. "Big cats hunt differently from wolves or bears. They don't just barrel straight ahead, jaws open, teeth bared. They track their prey for days. Toy with them. They wait for the right moment before striking. So if their first meeting is in a crowded room, chances are Darius isn't going to Change into his Lion and just go for the throat. He'll catch their scent, pick up the scent of his mate, and then—"

"And then the game of cat and mouse begins!" said Bis, rubbing her hands together and smiling wide, her brown face beaming with excitement. "Oh, this is so much fun! So what's the plan?"

"Just get them tickets to the circus," said Bart

with a grunt. "The circus tent counts as a crowded room, right? Boom. Done. Matchmaking accomplished!"

"Yes!" Bis shrieked, clapping her hands once and jumping up and down, her breasts and butt bouncing as her mate glanced at her with a hungry, naughty look in his eyes. "Mamma Mia! We'll Mamma Mia them!"

"What?" said Adam, frowning as he looked at Bis and then over at Ash, his mate. "What does that mean?"

"Mamma Mia," said Ash, her face lighting up with the same excitement. "The musical, silly! We send the bobcat sisters an all-inclusive trip to Morocco to see the circus! Tell them they won a contest or something!"

"All inclusive?" said Adam, his face darkening as his dragon tightened up inside. "You mean plane tickets, hotel rooms, VIP seats? Who the hell is going to pay for all of that!"

"I am!" shouted Bart, and in an instant he'd Changed into bear form and crashed out of the room, thundering down the stairs to the hidden underground levels of the castle.

"My vaults!" Adam roared, racing after the bear,

and once again almost getting trampled as Bart came bounding back up the stairs, his paws overflowing with bundles of hundred-dollar bills. "My money!"

"Simmer down, you miserly piece of birdmeat," growled Bart, holding the money in a bear-hug so tight that Adam the man couldn't even pull a single bundle away from him. "This is for a good cause."

Wisps of smoke rose up from Adam's nostrils and ears, but finally he calmed down and brought his dragon's hoarding instincts under control. Slowly a smile emerged on his tanned face, and he stepped back and slid his arms around his mate Ash.

"You're going to pay for suggesting this idea," he whispered to Ash, his hand patting her round butt as she turned red in the face.

Everyone laughed as Ash turned a brighter hue of red, burying her face in her hands as her mate lightly spanked her bottom once more. Then Bart Changed back to the man and glanced at his own mate, winking at her. "Speaking of ass," he said, his hungry gaze taking in Bis's strong curves. "Shall we . . ."

"We were *not* speaking of ass!" shrieked a mortified Bismeeta, her brown eyes going wide as Bart turned to her and began to take big, lumbering steps in her direction. "Ohmygod, do you ever think about anything else?"

Caleb cleared his throat, his own gaze resting briefly on Magda's natural hourglass shape before he smiled and blinked. "I think my boneheaded bear-friend is talking about the SSA—the Shifting Sands Agency. ASS in reverse."

"ASS backwards," said Bart, nodding very seriously. "See, honey? I'm talking business, not pleasure." He frowned and looked down at himself. "But speaking of boners . . ."

"OK, enough!" said Adam the Alpha, doing his best to keep a straight face. "I think we have a plan. And yes, I'll pay for the damned circus tickets. Now fade to black, please. Our role in this story is done for now."

"Speaking of rolling around . . ." Bart began to say as he lunged for his mate and swept her up in his arms while she shrieked in embarrassed delight. "See you chumps later," he called out as he barreled up the stairs towards their private chambers in one of the castle's towers.

Caleb shrugged, and then with the quickness of

his wolf he grabbed his own mate Magda, kicking open a side door and carrying her out.

Finally Adam turned to his mate, his eyes flashing with fire, heat, and single-minded purpose. "Time for your punishment, you bad, bad bear," he whispered, rubbing his hands together as the curtain slowly came down on the white castle floating on a sun-bathed island in the Caspian Sea.

And then the prologue was done, and it was time for Chapter One.

1
<u>THE BOBCAT TWINS</u>

"**D**ear Lacy and Tracy," said Lacy, raising her eyebrows as she read the letter out loud. She glanced up with an amused half-frown. "Hey! Did we sign up for some online contest?"

"Probably," said Tracy, rubbing her forehead as she stared at the empty Tequila bottle on the wooden coffee table of Lacy's sprawling ranch-style house on the outskirts of Denver, Colorado. She groaned as she reached for the two lipstick-stained shotglasses, pushing them away from her as she wrinkled up her nose. "Just so you know, I'm never drinking tequila again."

"You said that last week," retorted Lacy. "*Three* times last week, if I remember right. Not that I remember right, of course. Oh, shit, my head hurts. I'm never drinking tequila again."

Tracy giggled, and Lacy joined in until they were both in hysterics. Then Lacy cleared her throat pointedly as she looked down at her younger sister. Technically they were the same age (twins usually are), but Lacy had popped out first, and she never failed to remind Tracy of this claim to superiority. Still, they were two of a kind. Inseparable. They weren't identical—Lacy had brown hair to Tracy's golden locks. But they shared those same sharp eyes, round faces, and big butts.

Lacy chuckled as she glanced at the empty tequila bottle and thought about all the crap they'd pulled while drunk out of their minds. But this, she thought as she read through the letter once more . . . yes, this was weird. Different. Sure, they could've signed up for this thing while messing around on the Internet after downing shots and looking for funny cat-videos online. But it felt like a hoax, and the bobcat inside her tensed up as Lacy's sharp human mind begin to kick into high gear. She'd made her money on the Internet, running a web-design company that paid for her ranch-house, her three cars, a penthouse in Downtown Denver (which she rarely visited), and all the tequila she and her sister could drink. She was smart, and even when drunk out of her goddamn skull Lacy wouldn't have entered her name and address in some random Internet contest.

But this moron might've, she thought with a sigh as she watched her bobcat-sister writhe around on the floor, groaning and grunting like she was dying of some horrible disease. Lacy looked down at the contest material that had come via FedEx. The plane tickets were legit. And so was the circus: She'd looked it up online, and even though both the woman and the animal in her had risen up in anger when she saw that it advertised animals as part of the show, it was clearly a real circus, with a schedule that matched up with the plane tickets in her hand.

"What did we win?" said Tracy through a groan as she finally went up on her knees, sticking her large ass up in the air as she began to crawl towards the kitchen. "Breakfast, I hope. I need something warm and hearty. Preferably deep-fried."

"There are some jalapeno poppers you can microwave," said Lacy.

"Um, nope. I ate them last night after you passed out," said Tracy with a sheepish grin. She let out a soft, feminine burp and raised an eyebrow. "Yup," she said, nodding very seriously. "Definitely ate them last night."

"Eww! Gross!" said Lacy, swiping one paw at her sister as Tracy flopped down again on her back and started giggling. Soon both of them were once again giggling like fools, clearly still half-drunk, and Lacy just shook her head as she reminded herself that she'd always been the one in charge of their little two-person team. Tracy followed her lead. Tracy did what she said. Tracy trusted her twin's judgment.

And so Lacy blinked away the nagging feeling that something was off with this whole circus-contest thing and just made a decision.

"We won tickets to a circus," she said clearly and loudly. "And we're going."

"A circus?" said Tracy. "Like with trapeze and clowns? Jugglers and fools?"

"Trapeze and jugglers for sure," said Lacy with

a smile. "The clowns and fools will be present once you arrive."

"Haha," said Tracy drolly, rolling her eyes at Lacy. "Cheap shot." She paused for a moment, squinting and then closing one eye as she grabbed the tequila bottle and tilted it. "Speaking of shots, I think there's just enough for one more round. What say? Come on, sis!" She clapped her hands and sprang up to her knees like a cat, her face alert and earnest. She looked up at Lacy, her expression a mixture of pleading and pure mischief.

"All right," said Lacy after a sigh. "Serve it up. Because unless I'm mistaken, alcohol is banned in Morocco."

"Morocco?"

"Yup," said Lacy, raising her glass and downing it in one swift gulp. "Casablanca, Morocco."

"Casablanca!" said Tracy, slamming her empty shotglass back down on the table. "We gonna find our mates there? Alpha bobcats who claim us as their fated lovers?" She clasped her hands together and swooned comically.

"You know we're the last of the bobcat Shifters," said Lacy with a smile that was tinged with melancholy. "And we might well be the last Shifters in general. It's just the two of us. Like it always was. Like it always will be."

But even as she finished her sentence, she felt her cat move inside her, its restlessness making her frown. It had been years since she'd gained control of her animal. Both her and her twin were in firm control of their animals, in fact. They Changed back and forth at will. They controlled their needs when their animals went into heat, sequestering themselves in Lacy's isolated ranch-house just so they wouldn't be tempted at the bars and clubs in Denver.

Not that temptation had ever been a real problem, Lacy reminded herself as she smacked her lips and exhaled, the aroma of the strong tequila sending a warmth through her that calmed her animal down. Or drugged her animal into submission—she wasn't sure which one it was. No, neither of them had ever been really tempted by a man, even though there'd been plenty of offers dating back to middle school! It was strange, really. They were both healthy, hearty women of the mountains. And when their animals went into heat, the need to mate was strong, fierce, undeniable. When they were younger they'd go out to the bars and clubs, their animals sniffing the horny studs of Denver and then rejecting them with extreme disdain.

He is not our mate, her cat would reply pompously even though Lacy could sense the animal's soaring heat, feel her own feminine wetness soaking her panties like she couldn't control it. *We will not be touched by anyone other than our mate.*

It had been frustrating in the early years, feeling that conflict between wanting sex but still rejecting every man who came close. It had taken both sisters close to insanity at one point. It had made Lacy wonder if she was really in control of her animal. The creature seemed to submit to every command of the human. But on this one matter it wouldn't budge. It simply would *not* allow her to mate with a man!

He is not our mate.

He is not our mate.

He is not our mate!

The refrain had been whispered by their animals so often that Lacy had just put an end to it by deciding that both of them would lock themselves away in her ranch house when it came time for their animals to go into heat. That would show their bobcats who was boss. You want to reject every guy? Well, now there won't *be* any guys! Who's in control now, bitch?!

Lacy smiled as she walked over to the kitchen, reaching for the fridge to see what fryable items she could find for breakfast. Her gaze rested on the calendar marked up in pink highlighter, and she paused as she scanned it quickly. It was the calendar she'd drawn up to show when she and her twin were in heat. It had started off as a kinda-sorta joke, and in fact it had ended as a joke too. Both of them knew themselves and their bodies well enough to know when that time was approaching.

"That's weird," Lacy muttered as she counted out the days, flipping through the months until she got current.

"What's weird? Your butt?" said Tracy, gurgling with laughter. "Lacy's got a weird butt! Lacy's got a weird butt!" she yelped, slapping her own big thighs as she sang her ditty.

"Act your age, you moron," Lacy said with a raised eyebrow. She looked back at the chart and shook her head. "No, according to this chart, our animals aren't due to go into heat for at least another month. But I swear I feel . . . I mean, it feels like . . . I mean . . ."

He is our mate and we are ready for him, came her animal's whisper from inside her, and Lacy almost choked as she felt the excitement in her bobcat's voice. Excitement like she'd never sensed. Excitement that rippled through her core in the most delightfully ferocious way.

But it was also excitement that scared the crap out of her, because in that moment she got a sense that her bobcat had been waiting patiently for years, submitting to the human's every command as it stubbornly refused to budge on this one single thing:

Its mate.

Its fate.

Its destiny.

Lacy frowned as she sniffed the air, picking up the unmistakable scent of herself and her sister. It wasn't just her bobcat that was on the verge of going into heat—it was Tracy's too! How?! Why?! What?! When?! WTF?!

She glanced down at the two tickets in her hand. Tickets to Casablanca, Morocco. A city irrevocably linked to love and romance—at least in Western consciousness, thanks to that old movie. Then she took a breath and sniffed the air again, feeling her cat snicker in triumph, like it knew love was in the air, like it could smell the future, smell its own fate, its own mate.

2

Smells like Shifter, thought Darius the Lion as he raised his thick, muscular arms and then cracked his whip toward the raucous crowd. They cheered and clapped, whooped and whistled, making more noise than any group of animals could. Usually Darius loved the attention, the devotion, the awestruck faces of the humans as they watched him step fearlessly within a circle of fourteen lions, any of which could rip a man to shreds in a heartbeat. But today he was distracted by the scent coming to his finely tuned nostrils, making his lion rumble inside.

There are Shifters in the crowd today, Darius thought as he prolonged his traditional walk around the edge of the ring so he could scan the faces of those in attendance. He hadn't been around a Shifter in months—not since Murad the Black Dragon had disbanded the army and sent all of them back into human society. He blinked as he tried to remember what the Black Dragon had whispered to the Shifters in that deep, low voice that seemed to speak directly to the darkest part of their animals. Something about a mission, a duty to hunt, to stalk, to kill.

Darius could feel his lion moving inside him as he moved to the Southern end of the ring. The scent of Shifter blood was strong here, and he narrowed his eyes as he followed it like a trail. There. Sitting there in the third row, smiling like a goddamn fool.

"Well, I'll be damned," he muttered through his crowd-pleasing smile. "Everett the Tiger! What the hell?"

The two of them had bonded during the year

they'd spent together training in Murad's army, and Darius was glad to see him. But they'd both been sent to different parts of the world, hadn't they? What the hell was he doing in Morocco? What had drawn him here?

Slowly Darius turned back to his lions, all of which were waiting patiently for their master's commands. The beasts were like housecats when he was present, and although sometimes it broke Darius's mighty heart to see the majestic animals living in cages, he knew they were better off with him than with any other lion tamer. He was one of them and they knew it. They respected it. They even loved it.

Love, whispered his lion from within as Darius prepared to go on with the show.

"What?" growled Darius, gritting his teeth as he cracked his whip in the air, signaling to his lions to begin their stately parade around the ring.

Love is in the air, said his lion. *You smell it? You smell her? She is here. She is in heat. And she is ours. Take her now.*

Shut up you moron, Darius said to his animal. But then he picked up the scent. The scent of Shifters, but not his fleabag buddy Everett. This was feminine scent. Female Shifters. More than one.

Darius flicked his head to the right, and immediately he saw them: Two women sitting in the VIP section of the crowd. They were clearly sisters, twins perhaps—though not identical. They were both pretty, but Darius's gaze was unmistakably drawn to the woman sitting on the right, and the moment he looked into her eyes, his lion roared inside him like it was trying to burst out of him.

It took every ounce of Darius's willpower to turn away from the woman in the crowd, and even when he managed to move on with the show, he couldn't get the image of her face out of his mind. She had the brown eyes of a cat—sharp, focused, confident. She was clearly the leader of the two, and she was clearly his. There was no mistaking the way his lion had locked in on her like there was no one else in the world, in the universe. He'd heard about fated mates from Caleb the Wolf Shifter. He'd seen it at play with Bart the Bear Shifter and his mate Bis the Black Leopard. But he'd never believed it could be true for him.

The rest of the show went by in a flash, with Darius barely able to focus on his lions. His mind was spinning with the image of that woman in the crowd, and by the end of the show he could smell nothing but her heat, see nothing but her face, imagine nothing but taking her back to his cave and doing what came naturally.

"Darius the Lion Tamer!" came the ringmaster's voice through his stupor. "The King of the Ring! Give it up, ladies and gentlemen! Give it up for the King of the Ring!"

Darius forced a smile, blinking his eyes back into focus as he bowed for the crowd, cracked his whip once more over his head, and then led his lions back to their cages even as his own lion rumbled in disapproval.

But then just as he stepped behind the heavy velvet curtains, Darius heard screams from the crowd. Screams followed by the hissing of animals, the growling of big cats, the roar of a tiger, the rumble of his own lion.

"No!" Darius shouted, leaving his lions and breaking into a dead run, feeling his Change coming on as every hair on his golden mane stood up. Again snippets of what the Black Dragon had whispered to all the Shifters before sending them off came through: *Seek out the Shifters. Hunt them down. Kill them. Send their animals back to the Darkness so they can live forever, live free, free from the burden of human morals.*

Shit, was that why Everett was here? Had he been stalking his prey? Tracking his targets? Had he followed these women all the way down to Morocco? That was how big cats—tigers especially—hunted. Slow. Methodical. Toying with their prey until it was time to finish it.

Darius burst back out into the arena, knocking over the paunchy ringmaster, pushing aside the clowns, hurdling over the jugglers as he launched himself off the stage, Changing into his lion in mid-air, unleashing an unholy roar as he saw Everett the Tiger already in animal form, closing in on the two women.

Except it wasn't two women anymore. It was two bobcats, each of them Changed and ready, backed up against each other, their tails standing straight up, slowly twitching from side to side as they bared their claws and showed their teeth.

By now the arena was clearing out, and Darius landed on his paws, roaring at the tiger as he came up behind him.

"Are you insane?" he growled. "You're doing this here? In front of a thousand people?"

But Everett didn't even turn sideways towards Darius. His eyes were locked in on the bobcats, and Darius felt a chill go through him when he realized that Everett had singled out one of the bobcat sisters—the one who'd been sitting on the left. Instantly he understood that Everett wasn't hunting these women—not in that sense, anyway. He hadn't tracked these women here—not intentionally, anyway. His animal had led him here. Led him to his mate. Just like it had led these bobcats to *their* mates.

Excitement ripped through his lion as Darius stared at the bobcat on the right, the one he'd singled out by pure instinct, the one he *knew* was his, his mate, his woman, his destiny. Her brown eyes were narrowed and focused, and although he could tell she was highly aware of his presence, she was also deeply protective of her sister.

As she should be, whispered his lion as he slowly padded closer toward the standoff. *She and her sister are in danger.*

"Bullshit," Darius growled under his breath as he padded closer to his buddy the Tiger. "Everett isn't here to hunt. He's here to mate! Coming face to face with our mates has broken the hold that Murad's Black Dragon had on us, on our animals, on *you*. These bobcats have nothing to fear from us. So long as they accept that we are their mates, of course."

I didn't say they are in danger from us, whispered his lion.

"What?" said Darius, whipping his massive maned head upwards and sniffing the air. And then he smelled them: More Shifters. Dark Shifters. Dangerous Shifters. "Shit!"

Everett seemed to have picked up the scent at the same time, and then suddenly both big cats did an about face, their backs now turned to the two bobcats, the tiger and the lion crouching down, coiled like springs, ready to pounce, ready to protect.

"There's too many of them," Darius growled, keeping his voice low as he watched a group of dark, silent Shifters slowly descend from the back of the arena where they'd been sitting slumped in their seats like it was all still part of the show. They were all still in human form, which puzzled Darius for a moment—until he realized that their intention was to confuse their targets. They were hiding their animals until the last moment, and although Darius's lion could tell they were Shifters, it wasn't clear what animals they were! And that would make a big difference once the fight-ing started. It could mean the difference between life and death.

"No such thing as too many," growled Everett the tiger, his jaws almost dripping with drool as he pawed at the ground. "You can stand back with the girls if you're scared. I'll handle this."

"Yeah, right," whispered Darius, almost laugh-ing in delight as the adrenaline whipped through his lion's body. Hell, he'd *love* to fight right now! Get into it with his buddy by his side, rip those dark Shifters to ribbons as he protected his mate! But Darius knew he had to stay in control, sur-vey the situation, control not just his own ani-mal but the younger animal of his Tiger buddy as well. Everett didn't have the experience he did. Everett didn't understand that not knowing what kind of Shifter you're fighting puts you at a se-vere disadvantage.

It would be fine if it were just the two of them. But it wasn't just the two of them, Darius remem-bered as he picked up the scent of the women behind him. Again his lion could single out the scent of his mate clear as day, and he knew she would fight too. Yeah, her bobcat would join in the fray without hesitation, and there was no way in hell *she* knew what she was getting into fighting a Shifter who was all animal, all Darkness.

"Take her," Darius suddenly said, the answer coming to him out of the blue.

"I will, but now's not the time, Horndog," muttered Everett, turning his head and grinning through his tiger's maws. We'll take those dark Shifters first. I'll take the three on the left. You take the three on the right. First one done with his share gets to kill the two assholes in the middle."

Darius wanted to laugh again. But this wasn't the time. The dark Shifters were slowly walking down towards them, still in human form, still hiding their animals. Darius didn't recognize these guys from back in the desert, when Caleb had been training all of them. Were they new recruits? Was Murad somehow bringing more Shifters into the fold even while keeping his Black Dragon off the radar? Too many unknowns. You don't go into battle blind.

"I didn't mean *that* when I said take her," growled Darius, gesturing towards the ominous dark Shifters. He glanced over his shoulder at

the hissing bobcats. "I meant take her and *go*.
The bobcat. Your mate. Take her. Protect her.
Go now. *Now*!"

3

Lacy roared as she saw the tiger and lion turn towards her and her sister. Her head was buzzing with so much energy she wasn't sure what was going on. All she knew was that she was ready to fight—fight to the death to protect her sister. At first she thought she'd have to fight these two big cats. But then she'd seen the group of silent men slowly descend from the shadows of the arena like ghosts. She could sense they were Shifters, but there was something off about their energy. It scared her. It scared her animal.

She glanced at the lion, who was clearly the leader of the two big cats. His eyes were a deep gold, alive with intelligence, burning with the energy of his animal. He was looking right at her—indeed, he'd barely taken those gold eyes off her! It was only when those other Shifters showed themselves that he turned his massive lion's body away from her, crouching down like he was protecting her, like she mattered, like she was his.

"Take her and go," she heard the lion say. Then she saw the tiger whip around and head straight for Tracy, and Lacy screamed when she realized what was happening.

"No!" she roared, her bobcat ready to fight anyone and everyone. "You can't split us up! We go together! We fight together! We die together!"

But the tiger had already grabbed Tracy's bobcat by the scruff of its neck like it was a kitten, and just then Lacy felt the lion's massive jaws close around her own neck. His strength made her gasp; but it was strength combined with gentleness—the gentleness of how a lion picks up its cubs and carries them to safety.

"We *will* die together," growled the lion as he lifted her off her feet like she was a stuffed animal. "But not for another hundred years. Now stop struggling and do what I say."

Lacy hissed and tried to claw at his face, but a million years of evolution had made it so that a feisty cub couldn't turn and claw Daddy's eyes out when held by the scruff of her neck, and so finally Lacy just went limp in submission.

It shocked her, the way her animal had just submitted to the lion, and Lacy felt the heat rip through her sleek cat's body as its growl changed to a deep purr. It felt safe, protected, at ease even though all around them was chaos and danger! How could her animal let her down like that when her sister was in danger?! What the hell was happening?!

She is with her mate, purred her animal. *The tiger will protect your sister with his life. She is safest with him. Both of you are safer split up so the dark Shifters have to split up if they want to give chase. The lion is wise. Listen to him. Obey him. Submit to him. We are his, and the sooner you accept that, the sooner we can have babies.*

"Babies!" Lacy screamed as she felt the lion break into a dead run, heading for the tunnel leading out of the circus ring. Her sister was already gone, and Lacy still couldn't believe her animal was so damned calm about the whole thing! Could she even trust it anymore? Did nothing else matter now that it had met its mate? "My sister is gone! We're being kidnapped by a lion! Dark Shifters are on our tail! And you're purring in submission like a house cat and whispering about having babies?!"

"What's that about babies?" grunted the lion, barely even panting as it twisted and turned through the narrow spaces between the caravans and trailers of the circus. The entire area was abandoned after the madness of what had happened inside the big tent, though Lacy could smell the lions in their cages, the animals pacing nervously.

"Um, nothing," Lacy said hurriedly, trying desperately to stop her bobcat from purring like a horny sorority girl. "You can put me down now. We'll move faster without you carrying me in your mouth. Which, by the way, is completely unacceptable."

"Your animal seems to like it just fine," said Darius, a deep chuckle coming from his lion's throat, the rumble of his voice making her body vibrate in the most delightful way. "It's purring like a little kitten. I thought bobcats were supposed to be vicious and fierce."

Lacy tried once more to turn and swipe at the massive lion's face, but she couldn't do it while being held by the scruff of her neck. "Put me down and I'll show you vicious," she snarled playfully.

Playfully?! she thought as she felt her animal's heat wind through her again. Aren't we in danger here? Didn't my sister just get kidnapped by a Tiger Shifter? Aren't there some other very ominous Shifters chasing us down with murder in their dark eyes?

"Where is my sister?" she snarled, the playfulness leaving her as reality sank in. "She's just a kid. She needs me."

The lion grunted as it slowed its relentless run through the maze of caravans and cages. He cocked his head, his big golden ears standing straight up as he listened. Then Lacy heard him sniff the air before letting out a low growl and then finally dropping her onto the hard-packed dirt of the circus grounds.

"Ow!" Lacy growled as she landed on her ass,

her bobcat quickly jumping to its feet and facing the lion, who was maybe four times its size. "You'll pay for that."

"Maybe I will," said the lion, his wise golden eyes narrowing as he surveyed their surroundings. Finally he let out a long breath, like he was relaxing. "Those dark Shifters aren't following us. I don't know why, but they're hanging back. Retreating. It's strange, but I think we aren't in danger—for now, at least."

Lacy raised her snout and sniffed the air. She could smell Darius deep and clear, his masculine aroma filling her lungs, drugging her senses, making her weak at the knees. It took a moment for her to clear her head enough to pick up the other scents surrounding them, and when she managed to do it, she realized the lion was right. She could smell the other lions pacing in their cages. She could smell Darius—God, she could smell him! But no other animals. No other Shifters. Those mysterious Shifters had indeed retreated. Were they scared? Were they waiting for something? Would they be back?

"My sister," Lacy said again, blinking as she stared at the lion, the King of the Ring, this beast who made her feel funny inside, hot inside, like she wanted to roll over and just give herself to him even though she'd never rolled over for anyone in her life! "Where is she? She's probably terrified, and she needs her older sister."

"Older?" said Darius, his majestic face twisting as he looked her up and down. "You two looked around the same age, I thought."

Lacy blinked and cleared her throat. "Well, I'm older by three minutes."

Darius rolled his big gold eyes. "Talk about delusions of grandeur," he muttered.

"Excuse me?" said Lacy, her bobcat's neck-fur bristling. "Did you just make fun of me?"

"Your sister is as safe as she can be right now. She's with her mate, a trained warrior who will protect her with his life," Darius said, looking around once again like he was thinking, planning, deciding their next move.

"Did you just ignore my question?" Lacy demanded.

"There are bigger questions to answer right now," growled the lion, his eyes locking in on the distant cages of the circus lions. "And we're going to have to answer them before those dark Shifters come back for us."

"I have some questions of my own first," Lacy said.

Darius sighed. "All right. Fine. One question."

"*Three* questions."

"What am I, a genie from a lamp? *One* question!"

"OK, *two* questions then," said Lacy, feeling that playful smile come across her bobcat's jaws.

"This is not a negotiation," growled the lion, but he was grinning too, Lacy could tell. "I don't negotiate with kittens."

"Call me a kitten again," snarled Lacy, baring her sharp little teeth and slowly extending her claws. "Go on. I dare you."

"Kitten," said the lion without a moment's hesitation. "Kitten. Kitten. *Kitten!*"

With a hiss Lacy snapped at him, whipping her front paw across his chest with blinding speed. She gasped when she saw three red streaks form on the lion's beautiful golden fur, and then a rush of fear went through her when she looked into his eyes and saw the anger.

But the lion didn't strike back. Instead he calmly looked down at the blood trickling through his fur and grunted.

"The kitten wants to play? All right then," he growled slowly as the fear rose in her. The lion loomed above her like a mountain, and Lacy wondered if the beast would simply rip her to shreds right here and now! What the hell was she thinking?!

"Oh God, I'm so, so sorry!" she said, mewing up at him as she clumsily patted his wound with her paws.

"Ouch," he said, frowning and then swatting her paw away. "That isn't helping."

"Well, it's your fault," Lacy said firmly, once again surprised at herself for giving in to him so easily, for backing down, submitting. This wasn't her. She wasn't a . . . a pussycat!

"How is it my fault? I'm the one bleeding here," said Darius.

"I warned you not to call me a kitten. And you called me a kitten three times. Three violations. Three clawmarks. Seems fair."

"I'll show you what's fair," growled the lion, and a moment later he'd Changed to the man, naked and massive, his skin tanned to a golden brown, his long hair effortlessly flowing over his shoulders like it was indeed a mane.

Lacy stared up at the naked lion Shifter above her, her mouth moving like a fish out of water as she allowed herself to take in the sheer majesty of his presence. Arms as thick as tree-trunks, with veins popping out like roots. Pectorals hard and heavy like slabs of granite. A stomach lean and muscular, so cut that she could have counted the ripples on his abdomen. If she could still count, of course. Could she count? Nope, she couldn't. Not now that she'd glanced between his legs.

"Ohmygod," she gasped, suddenly realizing she'd Changed back to the woman. Her bobcat had retreated, making way for the human. She looked down at herself in panic, realizing that she was naked too, on the ground, her big thighs spread, boobs hanging off to either side, a naked Shifter four times her size standing above her with a cock the size of a pillar pointed right at her. "Oh, my *God!*"

Immediately she clamped her thighs together, covering her boobs with her arms as shame and desire rolled through her all at once. She was about to flip around onto her stomach and crawl away from under him, but then the thought of sticking her big ass up in the air stopped her.

"Relax, Kitten," whispered Darius, reaching down and brushing a strand of hair from her face. She could see her claw-marks on his bare chest. He'd already stopped bleeding, and she watched in wonder as the wounds slowly closed up, leaving not even the tiniest scar! "I'm not going to hurt you. Or do anything else to you. Not right now, at least. Not until you beg."

Lacy snorted, not sure if she was disappointed or insulted. "I don't *beg*," she snapped at him, but somewhere in the back of her mind came a disturbing image of her on her knees doing exactly what she said she never did.

"Your animal knows better," said Darius, slowly stepping away from her and walking over to a caravan. Lacy stared at his muscular butt moving as he kicked open the door, reached inside, and then emerged with a mismatched bundle of clothes. "Here. Put these on."

Lacy grabbed the clothes and sniffed them. They smelled surprisingly clean, and a wave of jealousy went through her when she picked up the scent of a woman on them. She narrowed her eyes up at Darius even as she realized how damned ridiculous it would be to actually get jealous. She didn't know him. And although her bobcat had muttered something about fated mates, her bobcat wasn't in charge—*she* was!

"You gonna put those on or do I need to dress you?" came his voice, and when she looked up Darius was standing above her, arms crossed over his chest, cock sticking straight out like he couldn't give a damn that it was so clear how freakin' aroused he was!

The emotions rolling through Lacy confused her, and she blinked when she realized that Darius was in complete control of himself, of his body, of his need. He wanted her, she could tell. But he wasn't going to take her even though she wouldn't be able to stop him!

Even though she wouldn't *want* to stop him.

He's going to make us beg, whispered her bobcat from inside, the little devil purring in the background like it was delighted to be watching the scene unfold. *Better find some knee-pads.*

"They belong to the ringmaster's wife," said Darius softly, his face glowing as he held back a smile. "She's like a mother to me. You have no need to be jealous. I'm your mate, and there's no one else. There can't be anyone else. That's what fate means."

Lacy stared up at this naked beast who was talking like he could read her mind, read her body, read her insecurities, her fears, her emotions. Had she been talking out loud? Was she so easy to read? Was she . . . was she really his mate?

If you have to ask the question so many damned times, then you already know the answer, hissed her bobcat, its whisper coming through with an edge. *Don't you feel it in your heart? Don't you feel it in your soul? How about between your legs?*

"Disgusting!" Lacy whispered, her eyes going wide at her bobcat's brazenness. But she could feel the heat in her body, smell her own feminine aroma between her legs. The lion Shifter could smell her too, she realized, and she blinked when she saw his jaw lock, the muscles on his abdomen tighten, his cock flex as his resolve wavered and he let himself look at her once more.

"You'd better cover up soon," he growled, taking a deep breath and forcing his gaze up from between her legs. "I'm trying to be a gentleman, but you're bringing out the animal in me."

"Typical male pig," Lacy said, feeling an odd sense of triumph when she realized that Darius wasn't really in as much control as he seemed. "Blaming a scantily dressed woman for tempting him."

Darius snorted. "You'll need to put on about three items of clothing before you'll qualify as scantily dressed, babe." He frowned as Lacy finally reached for the clothes. "And if I can't call you a kitten, then you can't call me a pig. Though I *will* call you Kitten."

Lacy closed one eye and looked up at him as she slipped the pink blouse over her head. She looked through the clothes and found a long black skirt that would fit her wide hips almost perfectly. "That's not a very good compromise," she said. "I'm supposed to do what you want, but you won't do what I want?"

"That's how it works when you're mated to a lion Shifter," said Darius with a shrug. He stepped back and helped Lacy up to her feet, his strong arms almost lifting her off the ground like she was weightless! "Ah. A perfect fit. Hopefully the ringmaster won't recognize those clothes when you meet with him. I don't think he will. He's half-blind, color-blind, near-sighted, and far-sighted."

"Wow. That's some diagnosis. You must have graduated at the top of your med-school class," said Lacy with a eye-roll. "Wait, why am I meeting with the ringmaster?"

"How else are you going to apply for the vacant position?"

"What vacant position?" said Lacy, frowning as she wondered if she'd missed something.

"Lion tamer," said Darius with a grin. He leaned in close, his breath warm against her smooth round cheeks as he whispered into her ear. "But be careful with that whip, Kitten. Or you'll get a taste of it yourself when the curtain drops."

Lacy just stared into his eyes that were like liquid gold, and she gasped when he stepped back from her and Changed into his lion with smooth, beautiful control. He tossed his mane back with a flick of his head, and quickly padded towards where she could hear the other lions pacing restlessly in their cages.

He won't leave his lions, she realized as her mind raced even as she had to almost break into a run just to keep up with Darius's lion-sized strides. And he's been outed as a Shifter, so he can't just continue being the lion-tamer. This place would turn into a media circus. Perhaps even worse. There'd be researchers and government officials all over the place! Perhaps the military would shut down the circus and try to take Darius so they could "study" him or whatever! Not a good idea to put a Lion Shifter in a cage. Not unless he chooses to be in that cage.

So what do I do? Leave his side and try to find my sister? What about those dark Shifters that followed us here and then stepped back into the shadows? My bobcat can fight with the best of them; but no way I can take on a group of male Shifters without Darius's help!

Are you done rationalizing why you need to stay by his side, you dumb human, sighed her bobcat. *The real answer is that he is our mate, our lion, our man. Your place is by his side, and you will obey him.*

"*Obey* him?! Ten minutes with a lion and you turn into a spineless kitten?" whispered Lacy to her bobcat as she hurried after her lion. In the distance she could hear voices, and she realized the circus folks were cautiously making their way back to their caravans. She still didn't understand exactly what Darius was planning, but there wasn't time for a long discussion. She had to trust him—if only because she needed him to find her sister.

Darius stopped right then, and Lacy bumped into him from behind, getting swatted by his tufted tail in the bargain.

"Unlock the big cage," growled Darius softly, his lion looking at her with those big golden eyes.

Lacy blinked as she looked past Darius and into the eyes of what looked like a million lions, all of them staring intently at Darius like he was in charge.

"I'm not unlocking that cage," Lacy whispered, feeling her bobcat tense up at the prospect of being surrounded by animals many times its size. Sure, these were just animals, and animals were no match for Shifters. But *fourteen* animals? Um, no.

"Trust me, Kitten," whispered the lion. He turned to the fourteen beasts in the cage, and in a firm, low voice said, "Sit."

And all fourteen lions sat down in unison, purring like overgrown house cats, all of them staring at their master as if waiting for his next command.

The voices were getting closer, and Lacy knew she had to make a decision. This sounded like a dumb idea, but what choice did she have? She didn't know what was going on. Hell, she didn't even know there were so many Shifters in the world! Darius was the only one she could trust right now.

So with a sigh she reached out and unlocked the cage, watching in silence as Darius stepped inside and took his place at the center of the group. He looked into her eyes and nodded, and she closed the cage and locked it again.

"Go," said the lion. "Come back tonight and tell the ringmaster that you heard he might need a new lion tamer. You can hide in my caravan."

Lacy nodded absentmindedly. It might look a bit suspicious for her to be standing there like a fool in front of the lion-cage. She turned to go, but then stopped. "Wait, won't they notice that there's an extra lion in here?"

"Nobody deals with the lions but me," said Darius. "I feed them. I care for them. The clowns and jugglers keep their distance. And the trapeze artists are too aloof to care."

"Trapeze artists too aloof? Hey, that's a pretty good joke for a circus animal," said Lacy. "Which reminds me, have you heard the one about—"

"Go!" rasped Darius, his golden eyes twinkling as if he wanted her to stay and tell him her silly joke even though this sure as hell wasn't the time.

Lacy smiled and nodded. But when she turned to go, she realized she had no idea which one was Darius's trailer. She was about to ask, but then she sniffed the air with her bobcat's sense of smell, and she knew she didn't need to ask.

She already knew his scent.
She'd never forget it.

4

"**F**orget it," grunted the ringmaster, squinting through a monocle that Darius had always suspected was fake. But the squint wasn't fake, and neither was his hesitation. "I already have a lion tamer. The best in the business. And business is gonna be up big time after that little display yesterday! Darius is one of those Shifter thingies! I've been getting phone calls all day from reporters around the world! The circus is sold out three times over! There's tickets being scalped for ten times the price!"

"Well, they're all going to be disappointed," said Lacy, standing straight and confident, her curves making Darius pant as he watched from the distance. "Darius isn't coming back. He has no interest in being a circus freak, which is what he would become after being outed as a Shifter."

The ringmaster snorted, adjusting his monocle and looking around the dark campsite. "Darius will be back. And the show will go on."

"What show? You've already cancelled tonight's program. Which means you've had to give refunds to thousands of customers. What happens if Darius doesn't show up tomorrow? Or the next day?" Lacy demanded. "Are *you* going to get into the cage with those lions?"

Darius let out a low growl, and immediately his fourteen lions joined in until it sounded like distant thunder rolling in. Perfect, he thought as the ringmaster's eyes went so wide his monocle fell off.

"No," he said hurriedly.

"How about your clowns?" said Lacy, taking a step closer and putting her hands on her hips.

"Maybe one of them can handle the man-eating beasts until Darius decides to come back."

The ringmaster snorted, but Darius could smell the little man's nervousness. The lions were a major attraction of the circus—especially since most circuses didn't use animals anymore. As for lion tamers . . . hell, they were hard to come by.

Speaking of hard . . ., whispered his lion as both man and beast watched their curvy, confident mate talk her way into being a goddamned lion tamer at a circus.

"Do not even go there," Darius muttered under his breath as he felt his lion's heat roll through him. It wanted to Change back, to give control back to the man, to let the man take his mate, claim her, mark her as his and his only. "We're going to have to stay in animal form."

For how long, grumbled his lion.

"As long as it takes to figure out what's happening," whispered Darius.

What's to figure out? said his lion. *She is our mate. You claim her, get her pregnant, and then we take care of our cubs. Next year we do the same. Ad infinitum. There! Easy! All figured out for you, King of the Ring!*

"Shut up," Darius grunted, straightening up

as he saw that Lacy was winning the argument and was now walking over to the big cage, the ringmaster following at a safe distance. "And get ready."

"Sit!" Lacy commanded through the bars of the cage, her voice clear and steady even though Darius could sense the nervousness in her.

With a low, almost inaudible growl, Darius repeated the command to his lions. Immediately they sat down on their bellies, all of them staring at Darius's lion, no doubt in their minds who was in charge.

"Roll over!" said Lacy.

Darius gritted his teeth and stared at Lacy through the bars of the cage. Roll over?! What was he, a puppy? Even a housecat wouldn't roll over on command!

"Roll over," Lacy said again, her brown eyes sparkling as she met Darius's gaze and held it.

Oh, you're gonna pay for this, Bobcat, Darius thought as he finally exhaled and repeated the command to his lions. He heard his lions clumsily roll over, their heavy bodies making the wooden floor of the cage creak, some of them releasing small growls of protest like they were saying, "What the hell is this, Darius?"

The ringmaster clapped in excitement, staring at Lacy and smiling. "I don't think I've ever seen Darius make them do that! What else can you do?"

Lacy shrugged. "Name it," she said.

"Make them stand on three legs!" squealed the round little man, rubbing his small hands together like a child.

"Stand on three legs!" said Lacy, spreading her arms out wide in a grand gesture like she was conducting an orchestra.

After a long hesitation, Darius ordered his lions to stand up and then balance on three legs. He could feel the anger boil through his proud lion's blood, and he wondered if the other lions had felt similarly humiliated when he'd led them into the ring and made them jump through flaming hoops.

"Now two legs!" shrieked the ringmaster. "And make them clap their front paws together! And jump like bunnies! Yes! Bunny-hops all around the cage!"

"There isn't enough place in the cage for all that," said Lacy hurriedly, and from the way she lowered her eyes and blinked, Darius could tell she'd picked up on his anger. "I can let them out if you like. Here. I'll just unlock this—"

"No, that's all right," said the ringmaster. He hurriedly took three steps back, smiling and shaking his head. "You've got the job. Until Darius comes back, of course."

"Of course," said Lacy, winking at the lion and then shaking the ringmaster's outstretched hand. "I can take over Darius's trailer, I presume?"

"Yes, go ahead," said the ringmaster. "It's yours. Until he—"

"Great," said Lacy, interrupting him and glancing over at Darius once more as a wicked smile broke on her pretty round face. "I'm going to do some re-decorating."

Wait, what did she just say? whispered Darius's lion.

"Wait, what did you just say?" Darius growled through the cage once the ringmaster had walked off.

"Oh, nothing," said Lacy, widening her eyes and shrugging. "Just going to move a few things around. And throw out everything else."

"My lair!" Darius roared as he watched Lacy pull open his trailer door and walk inside. "You do not mess with a lion's lair, Kitten. You don't know what you're doing. My lion can snap these bars like they're pretzel sticks."

"Go ahead," called Lacy from inside his trailer, where he could hear her rummaging through his drawers. A moment later she emerged at the door, a bundle of his old clothes in her arms. "But there's no way I'm sleeping in a trailer filled with T-Shirts from like twenty years ago. Look at this one! It's got rips and tears all the way down! There's no way you still wear this!"

"That has sentimental value!" roared Darius, pressing his massive head to the cage bars, his lion's heavy body making the metal bend. "Oh, woman, you are going to get it. You can't just walk into my life and . . . and . . ."

Darius roared in shocked anger as Lacy made a pile of his clothes on the hard ground outside the trailer, dousing it with a healthy squirt from the bottle of lighter fluid he kept on a shelf. She lit a long kitchen match, the flickering flame lighting up her face and eyes in a way that made Darius weak at the knees. He could see the defiance in this woman, the strength, the independence. She'd spent her life answering to no one, and this was her way of showing him that even though she

understood they were fated mates, she wasn't going to submit to his lion's dominance.

"You'll thank me later," she said, smiling at him
as she held the match over the pile of musty old
clothes.

"I'll *spank* you later," growled Darius, backing
away from the cage bars and pacing restlessly. He
knew he couldn't break through the cage, couldn't
lose control. His lions followed his lead, and he
couldn't allow himself to go berserk over a few
old T-Shirts. Well, *all* of his old T-Shirts. Shit,
she was going to pay for this when it was time.

Lacy's eyes widened at his threat. But Darius
picked up the scent of her telltale feminine musk
in that moment, and he knew that the image of
her bent over his knee, bare bottom upturned and
exposed, was making her hot, making her wet,
making her ready. Good, because he was going
to make her wait. Make her pant. Make her beg.

Make her submit.

"Whatever," he said finally, exhaling hard and
turning his back to her. "I don't care about those
clothes. "Burn them all."

"OK, cool," said Lacy cheerfully, and Darius
almost lost control when he saw her drop the
match, setting his entire wardrobe on fire as his

lion bared its teeth and dug its thick claws into the wooden floor of the cage. "Done! Well done, rather! Crispy!"

"You're insane," Darius whispered, shaking his mane and growling as he did a full circle and looked at her again. "Wild. Out of control." But at the same time he couldn't help but smile at her wildness, her defiance, the way she'd walked into his lair and decided to make it her own.

"On the contrary," she said, her face going serious as she stared into the flames. "I'm extremely sane and always in control. As for the wild part . . . well, I *am* a Shifter."

"Yes, you are," Darius said as he watched the flames light up her silhouette through the thin cloth of the black skirt she'd been wearing. He could see her strong hourglass figure, those wide hips, thick thighs, beautiful breasts. He could smell her scent—the woman and the animal. Hell, he could smell her heat too! But the human in her was clearly in control of her animal, of her lust, her need to be claimed by him. She wasn't going to just flop down on the ground and spread her legs for him no matter how much her bobcat mewed to be taken. Darius would have to win over the woman in her. Her animal was ready to be claimed, ready to submit, ready to be tamed.

The woman, however, was another matter, another challenge, a beast of a different nature.

"So you agree that I'm sane?" Lacy said, looking up at him through the flames.

"I agree that you're a Shifter who's in control of her animal," said Darius quietly. "And you're smart, I'll give you that. You know I won't break through this cage, won't risk people knowing that it's Darius in lion form, hiding amongst the animals. I'd be hounded by the press, the government, every research organization in the world. They'd put me in a *real* cage! Stick me with needles. Who knows what else."

"They'd kill you, that's what else," said Lacy softly, her brown eyes penetrating him with an understanding that shook the lion. "Because you'd kill any human who tried to put you in a cage, and once we start killing humans in public, there's no hope."

"No hope for what?" said Darius, frowning as he tried to interpret the depth of feeling in her words. Where was it coming from? Who was this woman? He knew she was his mate, and although his lion didn't care about anything else, Darius the man was suddenly deeply curious.

Lacy shrugged, rubbing her arms and slowly walking towards his cage. She sat cross-legged on the ground in front of him, so close he could smell every part of her, the scent making him want to roar in delight at being so close to his mate.

Suddenly a bolt of exhilaration ripped through Darius when he realized that in all the chaos of that day, he hadn't had time to bask in the simple joy of finding his fated mate! He'd been alone so long it seemed like that was his destiny, that the legend of fated mates was just a story, a myth, some crap his grandparents had told him to ease the grief of losing his parents at such an early age.

"Shifters never truly die," Grandma had whispered, brushing back young Darius's golden hair which was like a mane even before his first transformation.

"Not once they've found their fated mates, as your parents did," Grandpa had explained. "Yes, their bodies may die, but their souls are mated forever, and their spirits stay together through eternity. Your parents are sad to leave you, but they are happy together, complete together, forever together in a place of light and happiness. You should not grieve for them, Darius."

Darius had nodded as he listened to his grandparents, two old and proud lion Shifters who were the last of his kind—the last of *any* kind of Shifters, they'd told him.

"Fated mates," the young lion had said. "What does that mean?"

Grandpa had cleared his throat and looked at Grandma, an embarrassed smile breaking on his lips as if he wasn't quite prepared to have the birds-and-bees discussion with young Darius.

"You'll know what it means when you meet her," Grandma had said without hesitating, her gold eyes twinkling as she glanced at her own mate and then down at her grandson. "And so will she."

"No hope for peace," whispered Lacy through the cage, through Darius's daydream, through the smoke from his burning clothes.

"What?" he said, frowning as he rested his massive head on his paws and looked into his mate's eyes. It took a moment to remember what they'd been talking about, and then a chill went through him when it came back to him. "Oh, you mean if Shifters start killing humans in public. Yeah. My grandparents told me that's why there are so few Shifters left. So many out-of-control transformations, Shifters going feral, running wild.

And in a civilized world, when a beast runs wild you put it down."

Lacy's pretty face hardened as she listened. "Wait, you're saying our kind was wiped out by humans?"

"Not quite wiped out, Kitten," whispered Darius, smiling through his lion's jaws. "Soon enough our cubs are gonna be crawling all over the jungles of Africa."

Lacy blinked as the color rushed to her face, and Darius could tell she was still processing the flood of human emotion and animalistic need that flows when a Shifter meets her fated mate. Damn, if only they'd had time to consummate their meeting before circumstances put a set of iron bars between them!

"But those men . . ." Lacy said, swallowing and blinking again as if she was trying to stay on point. "They were Shifters, weren't they?"

"Yes," said Darius, sniffing the air to check for those dark Shifters's scent. No sign of them, which was strangely troubling. Who were they? They weren't part of Murad's army—at least not while Darius and Everett were there. Was the Black Dragon somehow recruiting more Shifters while in hiding? Or was something else going on?

"Why were they—"

"I don't know," growled Darius, finishing her question in his mind. "I don't know, Lacy. I thought they were here to kill you and your sister. Perhaps they were here to kill me and Everett. I just don't know."

"Why would a Shifter want to kill another Shifter?" Lacy said, her eyes going wide as she pulled her knees up close to her chest and leaned forward.

Darius snorted, shaking his mane as he smiled at her. "Were you always in control of your bobcat?" he asked quietly.

Lacy took a breath and furrowed her brow. "No," she said softly, a shadow coming across her face. "Tracy and I . . . we were wild during the early years following our first Changes. Luckily we had the open mountains of Colorado to run wild in, or else . . ."

She trailed off, and Darius narrowed his eyes when he saw the bobcat flash its wild streak through her gaze.

She is still wild, whispered his lion from inside, growling in approval. *And you will have to tame her, King of the Ring. Damn, it's going to be fun.*

"Or else what?" Darius said, forcing her to finish her sentence, to say it out loud, to acknowl-edge that every Shifter had a darkness in them—had *the* Darkness in them.

A shudder passed through Darius's lion as memories of the Black Dragon floated past him like it was from another life. Memories of his mis-sion: To hunt and kill other Shifters, send their animals back to the Darkness, increase the Black Dragon's dark power! His lion had been focused on that mission, accepting it like it had been hyp-notized, programmed, wound up and set into motion like a machine. But that was gone now! How? Why? When?

When she arrived, whispered his lion, and suddenly Darius made the connection—*all* the connections.

"Holy shit," he muttered as he thought back to that chaotic scene in the circus. "Those dark Shifters *were* there to kill you and your sister! But they didn't get to you in time! Once you and your sister came face to face with your mates, the dark Shifters backed off! It was like there was no point in killing you!"

"I don't understand," Lacy said, shaking her head and biting her lip. "None of what you're saying makes sense, Darius. I don't understand why Shifters are hunting other Shifters. And I don't understand why they'd *stop* hunting me if . . . when . . . I mean now that I'm . . . we're . . ."

Darius turned his head sideways and raised a lion-brow as he listened to this confident, articulate woman who'd just talked her way into a lion-tamer's job now stammer and stumble on saying what was glaringly obvious: That they were mates! *Mates*!

"Mated Shifters are mated forever, through space and time, life and death," said Darius, repeating the words his grandparents had whispered to him all those years ago. "Which means that if you kill a mated Shifter, its animal *doesn't* split from the human soul and return to the Darkness! That's why the Black Dragon has to kill Shifters *before* they meet their mates!"

"Black Dragon?" said Lacy, shaking her head as her frown cut deeper. "Is that as bad as it sounds?"

"Yes," said Darius. "Sheikh Murad. Dragon Shifter gone feral. Wild. All dark."

"I saw some footage of a dragon Shifter from a couple of years ago," said Lacy, her eyes widening. "It burst through some coffee shop in Milwaukee! Destroyed the building and flew off with a woman in its talons! The media dismissed it as a hoax, but there's no doubt *something* destroyed that building."

"That was Adam Drake, the green-and-gold dragon," said Darius. "Sheikh Murad's son. The only creature alive that can kill the Black Dragon."

"Well, that sucks," Lacy said, trying to smile even though Darius could see her sharp mind putting together the bits and pieces of information. "Killing your own father is probably a bummer."

Darius laughed, shrugging his heavy shoulders as his lion's body trembled. "Yeah. Total bummer. But maybe he won't have to kill Papa."

"Oh, *you're* going to kill a feral Black Dragon on the warpath?" said Lacy, smiling as her voice took on a teasing lilt. "Talk about delusions of grandeur. Not to mention that you're currently in a cage."

Darius looked around and sighed. "Oh, right. Well, maybe you'll have to save the world, then. Wake me up when it's done, will ya?"

Lacy laughed, rocking back and forth as she hugged her knees tighter and looked into his eyes. God, she's beautiful, Darius thought as he felt his lion's heat roil his blood, bringing out the man in him, the need in him, the need to take his woman, claim his mate, tame this curvy bobcat and fill her with his seed!

Mine, he thought again. Beautiful and mine! *Mine*!

He wanted to stand up and roar, let every beast in the jungle know that the lion had found its mate and all was right with the world! But he knew that all wasn't right with the world, that although he'd met his mate and had spontaneously been released from whatever hold Murad's Black Dragon had on him, he had a responsibility, a duty, an obligation. He couldn't just break through these bars, claim his mate, and disappear into the jungles of Africa. He wasn't just an animal. He was a man. A leader. A goddamn *king*!

And she is my queen, he thought as he studied her face, watched how her chest moved from each breath she took, listened to her heart beat in time with his.

My queen.

5

"Behold! I now introduce the *Queen* of the Ring!" said the ringmaster in a surprisingly powerful stage-voice as Lacy stepped into the middle of the circus ring, a rush of nervous energy ripping through her as the crowd hissed and booed and called out Darius's name.

We want to see the freak! called the crowd.

Bring out the Lion Shifter! roared the rabble.

Show us your boobs! hooted some hooligans who were probably drunk and definitely American.

Lacy heard Darius growl in anger at the assholes who'd shouted that last line, and she almost turned to the billowing purple curtain behind which the lions stood ready to come out at her command.

"You know what?" growled Darius through the cacophony of crowd noise, his voice coming through so clear that Lacy wondered if everyone else could hear him. "I'm just gonna rip a couple heads off. It'll just take a minute, and people will settle down after that."

"No!" muttered Lacy, almost laughing as both she and her bobcat imagined her lion-mate bounding off the stage and using his powerful paws to knock the heads off the group of what appeared to be drunk American college students who thought they were at a strip club. "I got this."

"Better hurry," growled Darius from behind the curtain, his voice low but still coming through clearly to her. "Or else I'm gonna teach this new generation some fucking manners."

"Language, please," said Lacy from the side of her mouth. She raised her arms and walked to the edge of the stage, standing right in front of

the rowdy group of Americans. "Remember, when
they go low, we go high."

"Did you just quote Michelle Obama to me?"
whispered Darius, and Lacy chuckled as she wondered if everyone else could hear the talking lion
too. Apparently not. It was loud enough in the
arena. "All right then, Queen of the Ring. Let's
see how you handle the crowd. I'll give you ten
seconds before I start eating people."

"How about staying quiet for like ten seconds
so everyone doesn't hear you, all right?" Lacy
whispered back before standing as straight as she
could at the edge of the ring, holding her arms
upright like she was commanding the crowd to
simmer down. Incredibly, the audience responded, and Lacy felt a rush like she'd never felt as she
surveyed the upturned faces of people from all
over the world.

I could get used to this, she thought as she
flashed a smile and kept her feet together. She'd
always been confident in front of people, com-
fortable with her curves, and she smiled down at
the drunken morons in the third row and widened her eyes.

"Did I hear you guys volunteer to come up on
stage?" she said. She waited for just a fraction of

a second—enough to take some pleasure in the looks of panic as they stared back at her. "Ladies and gentlemen, we have some volunteers! Come on up, guys! Everyone, give our volunteers a hand!"

The crowd burst into raucous applause, drowning out the feeble protests of the boisterous drunks, who'd gone awfully quiet suddenly.

"It's all right, guys," Lacy said cheerfully as she waited for them to meekly step onto the empty stage and stand there blinking nervously in the spotlight. "I already fed my lions earlier today."

The crowd roared with laughter, and Lacy turned and cracked her whip. Immediately all fifteen lions burst out through the curtain, Darius leading with his head held high, golden eyes riveted on his mate, mane shining under the spotlight.

My God, he's beautiful, Lacy thought as her bobcat purred and mewed inside like it really was a kitten—*his* kitten. It took a moment for her to focus back on the scene, and when she saw the color drain from the faces of her reluctant volunteers, she wondered if she'd made a mistake.

But Darius was calm, and his lions followed their master's lead with precision as the lion Shifter did a full round of the circus ring, all the animals in lockstep. They stopped at Lacy's command, and when she raised her arms again, they all sat on their haunches and stared at the terrified volunteers.

Lacy relaxed, smiling and turning to the crowd. "What do you guys say?" she called out. "Should we feed them to the lions? Yay or nay?"

She raised her right hand, thumb up in the air like she was the empress of Rome and this was the coliseum. The crowd hooted and hollered, and Lacy felt a strange chill go through her when she sensed an underlying wildness, like they really *were* calling for blood!

"Something's not right," Lacy muttered, blinking as she felt her bobcat suddenly thrash inside her like it was trying to get out, trying to come forth, like it was getting whipped up into a frenzy just like the crowd. Her vision blurred as she stared out into the crowd, scanning the faces of humans who seemed no better than animals right then, their faces twisted, mouths wide open, teeth bared, eyes narrowed. "What's happening, Darius?"

But Darius didn't answer, and when Lacy turned to her mate she saw that the lion was standing rigid like a statue, gold eyes focused on a spot deep in the crowd. She followed his gaze and immediately saw them: Those dark Shifters who'd showed up the other day! They were back! Or perhaps they'd never left!

Lacy had to almost scream at her bobcat to control its need to burst forth, and she could sense the other lions begin to move from their obedient positions. Darius was wholly focused on those other Shifters, and Lacy knew that her mate's protective instincts were consuming him. He sensed danger to his mate, and nothing else mattered to his animal more than protecting her.

Lacy herself was feeling torn, and the chants of the crowd simply raised her bobcat's anxiety as the drunk buttheads in the ring shifted on their feet and stared at the restless lions surrounding them.

Breakfast for the beasts! howled the bloodthirsty crowd like they'd lost their minds.

Lunch for the lions! they yelled like it was all a crazy game.

Thumbs down! they howled like this was ancient Rome and she was Nero.

From the corner of her eye Lacy could see Darius slowly moving toward the edge of the ring, his attention completely focused on those dark

Shifters who seemed to be doing nothing but sitting in the crowd in human form, their faces expressionless and zombie-like, their eyes unblinking but focused . . .

Yes, focused—but not on Darius or me, Lacy realized as she followed their line of sight and saw that they were staring at one of Darius's lions: a young male with a streaked, ragged mane.

"No!" Lacy whispered as she felt the poor dumb animal tense up as if those dark Shifters were controlling it. "Darius! On your left!"

Darius turned just as that young lion rose up and roared, launching itself with all the power of its muscular haunches . . . launching itself with jaws wide open, savage teeth glistening with drool, eyes blood-red with rage that seemed to come from somewhere outside it.

Lacy screamed, and then she lost control of her bobcat, her animal bursting forth as it sensed danger to its mate from behind. It was only then that Lacy realized the young lion wasn't attacking Darius.

It was attacking the trembling humans she'd called up into the ring!

Terror and shock whipped through Lacy as her bobcat prepared to meet the young lion in mid-air. She'd fought with her sister before when in animal form; but those fights had been in play, even though they'd both come away with some serious scratches and even a few bites. As a Shifter she was almost certainly stronger than a regular animal, but this lion was no joke. It looked seriously wild, mad, feral. Those dark Shifters were doing something. She didn't know what, didn't know how, didn't know why. She just knew it was happening.

Lacy closed her eyes as she felt her bobcat's jaws open wide as it prepared to attack the feral lion. But then she felt the wind knocked out of her, and she hissed in shock as she landed on the heavy carpet of the ring, her bobcat twisting in the air so she could land on all fours, ready to spring back into action.

But there was no need, because Darius's lion had heard her warning and with lightning speed had jumped between Lacy and the lion, knocking her out of the way and twisting his massive body in the air so he could use his front paws to push the feral lion away from the screaming drunks, who were wailing like they'd already been ripped down the seams!

"Stand down!" Darius roared to his lion, but

the feral beast was too far gone, and it found its balance and made another rush at the vulnerable humans. "Don't make me do this!"

Lacy was almost in tears as she tried to push away the thought that it was she who'd called these poor assholes up on stage, putting them in harm's way. If they were killed in front of a thousand people . . . people who now knew that Lacy was a Shifter . . .

The thought froze her as her intelligent human mind keep spinning, replaying the way those dark Shifters had somehow taken control of the lion and made it attack the humans. In front of her Darius was fighting the lion now, both beasts at each other's necks, claws out, teeth bared, manes flying like battle flags.

She'd expected the crowd to have panicked and headed for the exits, but when Lacy heard a fresh round of cheers rise up, she was startled to see that most people were standing, fists pumping in the air like this was all part of the show!

With a roar Darius bit down hard on the feral lion's thigh, sinking his sharp teeth into the muscle and pulling the lion down to the carpet. But the feral beast barely even reacted, turning its body and slashing Darius across the back with its claws, drawing fresh blood that rolled down his golden fur in streaks.

"No!" Lacy screamed, leaping at the young lion, her bobcat going right for the feral lion's throat. She had no choice. She was going to put this lion down, audience be damned!

"No!" came Darius's roar, his paws knocking her off her feet once more. "We can't! It doesn't know what it's doing. We can't put it down! Help me control it!"

The lion is talking! shouted someone from the crowd as gasps rose up through the cheers.

It's Darius the Shifter! cried someone else.

Shifters versus animals! howled a third person from the rabid crowd.

Lacy managed to control her bobcat just in time so her jaws clamped tight before she landed on the young lion. With her hard head she butted the lion square in the nose, which seemed to faze it long enough for Darius to take over once again. A moment later Darius had brought the young lion to its knees, forcing it to roll over and raise its paws in submission.

"Run, you morons," Lacy hissed at the cowering, blubbering idiots who were still on the stage, hugging each other and wetting their pants like children. "And mind your manners next time, OK?"

Darius looked up at her, a grin emerging through his lion's open jaws. Lacy grinned back, even though there was nothing remotely funny about what had almost happened here. But she couldn't deny the rush of euphoria that flooded her senses from the action, the joy of teaming up with her mate, the primal pleasure of releasing her animal and letting it do what came naturally: jump, snarl, hiss, fight!

"You should . . . go," said Darius in a low voice. He growled once more at the now-calm young lion, glancing down at its injured thigh.

"What do you mean? We should *both* go, Darius! Everyone knows you're a Shifter too now!"

"I can't leave my lions, Lacy," Darius said. "They'll put them all down! Or send them to zoos!"

"And what do you think they'll do with you? With us?" Lacy snapped back at him. "You think the show will just go on like normal? Everything's changed, Darius. The cat's out of the bag. The world knows that Shifters exist, and nothing's going to be the same again. We have to go. We'll come back for your lions. They're protected species in Africa. And with all the media coverage, the Moroccan government isn't going to just come in and shoot them dead! There'll be too much outrage with the whole world following the story."

Lacy glanced up and scanned the crowd. She looked for those dark Shifters, but they were gone. Somehow that didn't surprise her. Had they already accomplished what they came for? Did they simply want Darius and Lacy to expose themselves as Shifters in front of a thousand iPhone cameras?

"Please," she said to Darius. "If you stay here, you'll be put in a cage before any of your lions are! You'll become a test subject for the government!"

Darius grunted, slowly stepping back from the fallen young lion and turning to Lacy. "And you think I'll sit there quietly while they stick needles in my butt and attach electrodes to my nipples?"

"Those are some interesting thoughts on what it means to become a test subject," Lacy said with a smile. "But no, I *don't* think you'll let anyone do anything to you! That's why we need to run! Or else it'll be *you* killing humans on camera! Don't you see!"

"I'm in complete control of my animal," Darius grunted, the pride in his tone frustrating Lacy almost as much as it aroused her. "I will control it all. Get out of here, Lacy. I can't worry about you along with all this."

Lacy exhaled hard, and then she just sat down on her haunches and looked up at him, her bobcat licking its snout and then nonchalantly beginning to groom itself.

"What are you doing?" growled Darius. "I told you to get out of here!"

"What does it look like I'm doing? I'm grooming myself," said Lacy. "Oh, look at that obstinate tuft of fur sticking up like a mohawk! How embarrassing! There we go. That's so much better." She looked up at him, feeling the stubbornness rise up from the woman in her. Her bobcat was more than happy to groom itself, its mate by its side. It couldn't give a damn about media coverage, iPhone cameras, or anything else really. "You could use a little grooming yourself. Want me to—"

"I said *go*!" roared the lion, turning and facing Lacy head on, its deep rumble sending shivers through her.

"My, we have a temper, don't we?" said Lacy, her voice lilting and sickeningly sweet in a way that she could tell was driving Darius nuts. "That's going to be a problem if we're to be mates, you know."

"We *are* mates," growled the lion. "And you will do what I say, when I say, without argument."

Lacy snorted, closing one eye and holding up her right paw. "Is this toenail chipped? Do you know of any good nail salons in Casablanca?"

Darius almost lost his mind, and his eyes glazed gold like fire as he dug his claws into the thick carpet like he was doing everything he could to not launch himself at her and force her to submit.

"In case it isn't clear," she said firmly, holding his gaze with all the confidence she could muster even though her bobcat wanted to lower its eyes and give in to its powerful mate, "I'm not going anywhere without you. You want to stay here? Fine. But I'm staying too, and there's really nothing you can do about it. Sorry."

"Lacy," the lion whispered. "You're not making sense. You're—"

"Oh, so if I don't do what you say, it means I'm a hysterical woman who's not making sense? Maybe I have my period! That's probably why I'm talking hysterical nonsense!"

Darius snorted in surprise. "Are we fighting?" he said, turning his head to the side and closing one eye. "Because that's generally not a good idea when your mate is a lion, you know."

"My mate is a moron, far as I can tell," Lacy muttered. "Hear that? Jeeps. Trucks. Armored vehicles. That's the Moroccan military pulling up outside. The window is closing, Great King." She gestured at the billowing velvet curtain behind them. "And there's the door. I suggest we use it."

Darius took a long, deep breath, his gold eyes transforming as Lacy saw the anger slowly melt away, leaving behind what she swore was admiration. It almost embarrassed her, and she finally blinked and looked down, her bobcat purring from the unspoken approval of its mate. God, who knew her cat would turn out to be such a pussy in front of its mate! Good thing Lacy the woman was anything but!

"Stay close behind me," whispered the lion, narrowing its eyes as the voices of the Moroccan military officers came through to them. The crowd had been ordered out of the arena, and soon enough the place would be swarmed by men with guns—men who were dangerous simply because they'd be scared at dealing with something they didn't understand. "We get in a fight, you head for the jungle."

"Jungle? You know that Morocco is mostly desert," Lacy said as the lion broke into a brisk run and her bobcat raced after him. "We'll have to head south to find jungle."

"Then South it is," roared the lion as they burst through the velvet curtains and tore through the winding pathways of the circus village, their Shifter-animals moving like streaks of lightning, like bullets of pure cosmic energy. "Stay close, Kitten. Stay close."

6

"**A**ny closer and I won't be able to breathe," Lacy gasped, her breath warm against Darius's bare chest.

Darius grinned as he looked down at his mate cuddled into his body. She was turned on her side, the curve of her hips looking smooth and beautiful as her thick thighs shuddered with the rumble of the freight train they'd hopped aboard so they could head South, deeper into Africa, in search of the safety of its vast, wild jungles.

"Desert nights are cold," said Darius. "I just don't want you to get sick."

"Then you should have listened to me when I said we should stop and get some clothes," said Lacy, frowning up at him even though a smile was pulling at her lips.

"We're never wearing clothes again," Darius said. "We're heading to the jungle, away from the fetters of human civilization. Besides, you burned all my clothes, remember?"

Lacy giggled. "Why did you have so many T-Shirts with heavy metal band logos on them? What are you, a seventeen-year-old angst-ridden kid from the suburbs?"

Darius dug his fingers into the soft flesh of her side, making her squirm. "That's prejudicial," he said, his breath catching as he felt his cock move against her bare skin. He'd been hard for hours, but somehow he'd been content to just lay with his mate, feel the softness of her smooth skin, marvel at how the contours of her body seemed to fit so perfectly with the ridges and hard lines of his massive, muscled frame. Images of the moment when he'd finally peel her off him, flip her over, and claim her the way his animal wanted were pushing through in his mind, but he pushed back against them. He could smell Lacy's wetness, feel the heat between her legs, sense her desire to be taken. But somehow that made him want to hold back even more. This woman challenged him, and he wanted her to beg, wanted her to get on her knees, raise that magnificent ass, and plead to be taken.

"Angst," Darius whispered, leaning close to her face, his breath making the loose strands of her brown tresses shiver. Slowly he cupped her ass with his big right hand, squeezing firmly as he felt her breath quicken, her heart beat faster, that telltale musk of her wetness rise up to him like a beacon. "Is that what you're feeling right now, waiting for me to claim you? *Yearning* for me to claim you?"

Her breath caught again as he spoke, but she just blinked and then looked at him with wide-eyed innocence. "Nope. I'm just fine. How about you?"

Darius grinned. "Oh, I'm just chilling. Thinking about baseball."

"Is that right?" Lacy said, her round cheeks blushing bright red as the setting sun shone through the open door of the freight train car.

"Yup."

"That must be why it feels like there's a bat pressed up against me," Lacy whispered. She broke eye contact and blinked rapidly, as if she was genuinely shocked at what she'd just said.

Darius laughed as he squeezed her ass tighter, feeling his cock go to full mast. Who was this woman?! She had so much boldness, courage, and defiance. But she also seemed shy, bashful, almost ashamed when it came to matters that should seem so natural. Matters of sex. Mating. The body.

"So you got a guy waiting for you back in . . . wait, where are you from again?" Darius said.

Lacy shook her head against his body. "Colorado. And no, there's no guy. Why would you ask me that? Is there a woman in your life? Ohmygod, there is, isn't there? Who is it? One of the trapeze artists? The bearded woman from the freak-show? One of the clowns?"

Darius laughed. "*You're* the clown," he said, grunting as he pushed his nose against her open hair and sniffed. "You even smell like a clown."

"I *smell* like a clown? Wow, you are really taking romance to a new level here. Get away from me, you freak."

"Sorry. No. My lion won't allow it. We're going

to be joined together at the hip for all of eternity."

"Sounds uncomfortable," Lacy said with a giggle and a snuggle. "How will we walk if we're joined together at the hip?"

"There'll be no walking," said Darius firmly. "Just rolling around in the jungles, our hips pressed against each other as the animals stare at us."

Lacy giggled again. "You like having an audience, don't you?"

"Love it," said Darius. "I love being up there in the spotlight." He paused and took a breath, looking down at his mate. "I think you like it too."

"I do not," she said quickly. But then she scrunched up her face and closed one eye. "Well, maybe I do. It's kind of a rush to stand up in front of a crowd."

Darius nodded as he thought back to how his mate had stood there in the ring, riling up the crowd. But then his smile tightened when he remembered how that crowd had turned into something like a bloodthirsty mob! What the hell had happened?! It had to be those dark Shifters—Murad's Shifters—who'd done that. But how? Why?

"What are you thinking?" came Lacy's voice over the sound of the train rattling along the tracks.

"You know what I'm thinking," he said softly. "And I don't want to be thinking that. I want to be thinking of nothing but us. The two of us roaming free in the jungles of Africa, raising our cubs, strutting through the land like a king and queen. The way nature intended. We're animals, Lacy. Why can't we just live like animals?"

"Because we're not just animals, and you know that," Lacy said against his chest. "We're blessed with human emotions, but that's also a curse sometimes. It means we can't turn away from the world. We won't turn away from the world."

"I know," Darius said. "And that's why I love you."

"Wait, what?" she said, her heart pounding so loud he could hear it like a drum. "You . . . you love me?"

Darius blinked as he felt his own heart hammer away inside him, its beat in perfect rhythm with his mate's. He hadn't planned to say the L word. Hell, he didn't even realize he'd said it! It just came out, and now it was out there!

Suddenly Darius felt a strange vulnerability, something he'd never felt in his entire life! He'd never experienced any teenage crushes, never had to deal with the pain of unrequited love, never basked in the joy of being in love with someone who felt the same way. And here he was, holding a woman in his arms—a woman that his lion knew was his mate—and he was terrified!

"No, of course I don't love you," he said quickly. "I mean, we barely know each other."

"Right," said Lacy, blinking as the color drained from her face like she was as scared as he was. "I don't love you either. We can't be in love. It takes time to fall in love. Six weeks at least."

"Six weeks? Is that official?"

"I read it in *Cosmo*," said Lacy with that wide-eyed look of playful innocence. "It takes six weeks of daily contact to fall in love."

Darius grunted as he slowly massaged her large rump. "What if we squeeze six weeks worth of contact into one day? Would that make us pass the love test?"

Lacy giggled, and then she gasped as Darius slowly parted her rear crack with his strong fingers, keeping his hand there as his cock throbbed against her thighs. "Yes, but I don't know if that's the sort of contact *Cosmo* was talking about. I don't know if . . . oh, God, Darius! That feels . . . it feels . . ."

"Feels like love?" Darius whispered with a wicked grin as he slowly traced his fingers around her circular rim from behind.

"You're sick," she moaned. "Perverted. There's no way you're going to . . . oh, that's . . . that's . . . *oh*!"

Darius groaned as he slowly pushed his middle finger into her rear hole, and he trembled as he felt Lacy's thighs spread like she couldn't hold them together any longer. Her scent was so strong in the cool evening air that Darius's vision blurred, and he rolled on top of her, his finger driving deep into her from behind as his weight pressed down on her body.

"You know," he whispered, blinking as he tried to focus on her face. Slowly his vision returned, and he smiled when he saw how her eyes were rolling up in her head as the heat rippled through her body. "I haven't even kissed you yet."

"That's OK," she muttered. "I didn't expect you to be a gentleman."

Darius grinned wide, bringing his lips so close to hers that he could almost taste her. He curled his middle finger inside her, making her groan and open her mouth wide. "Wait, this isn't gentlemanly behavior? Oh well, what can you do.

I'm just a circus freak. A travelling sideshow." He paused as his smile faded. "An animal," he whispered.

His lion roared inside him, and Darius felt the energy of his beast rip through every fiber of his being, roiling his blood until his head was spinning. He wanted to flip her over and take her so hard her screams would be heard all the way across the Serengeti. But for some reason he was holding back, as if he sensed he needed to start slow with her. Why? He could sense her bobcat's heat, smell Lacy's need, feel her wetness oozing from her slit as he pressed his cock lengthwise against her. Why was he holding back? She was already submitting to him. He could feel it. He could take her any way he wanted. In the three days he'd known her he'd already fantasized about spanking her ass, spreading her wide from behind, making her hiss and snarl for him while he filled her again and again with his seed. So why was he—

"Darius," she whispered, her eyelids fluttering as she looked into his eyes. "I need to tell you something. I . . . I'm . . . oh, God, it's so embarrassing! I'm in my thirties, and I've never . . . never had sex before! I'm a . . . a . . ."

"I know," said Darius without hesitation. And

he did know. His body knew. The man inside him knew.

"You know? How?"

"Because I am too," he whispered, a shudder passing through him when he revealed what he'd never said out loud to anyone—not even himself. "I'm yours, Lacy. I always was, even before I knew you existed. I'm yours, and you're mine. Mine, you hear?"

And then, as the sun dipped below the horizon and the train chugged and rattled its way across the Kenyan border, he kissed her. He kissed her softly, slowly, with a tenderness that somehow contained all the power of his lion. He kissed her. By God, he kissed her.

7

His kiss sent shivers through her body, and Lacy felt her bobcat roar inside her as it retreated to the far corner of her consciousness, content to let the human woman enjoy the moment. And what a moment it was: The feeling of his thick finger inside her rear while his tongue slowly pushed into her mouth was a dizzying mixture of opposites, like he was dominating her while at the same time submitting to her, being rough and tender all at once, giving her what the horny animal needed while making sure the woman in her felt protected, safe . . . loved?

She moaned softly as she kissed him back, letting her mouth fall open as Darius pressed his heavy body down on hers. The rhythm of the train felt in perfect harmony with their hearts, and she moaned again and then gasped as she felt her mate's hunger for her begin to rise.

It took a moment for her to realize the strangeness of what they'd just admitted to one another: That they were each other's first! It seemed weird, but Lacy knew that was just the human brain talking, the brain of a woman who'd been reading *Cosmo* since she was eleven years old, a woman who of course understood that sex was natural and should be had by every consenting woman, as much and as often and with as many different partners as she chose.

Then why hadn't she chosen anyone?

Why hadn't *he* chosen anyone?

"Is this real, Darius?" she whispered, her eyes suddenly going wide as a terrible fear whipped through her that perhaps they were dead or this was all a dream or a spell or some power that those dark Shifters were using on them. "Are we real?"

"What are you talking about?" Darius muttered, drawing back from the kiss and looking deep into her eyes. "This is the *only* thing that's real, Lacy. The only thing guaranteed for a Shifter. His fated mate. Everything else in our lives is just window dressing, just the universe playing its games as it brings us together. Now. Here. Forever."

Lacy smiled as she felt that fear dissolve with his words, felt herself dissolve into his eyes of liquid gold, felt her body yearn to merge with his, take his seed, bear his cubs. "That's pretty romantic for a circus freak," she whispered. Then she felt his finger curl inside her rear and she gasped, her eyes rolling back in her head. "But that . . . that's most certainly not!"

"You can take the freak out of the circus, but you can't take the circus out of the freak," said Darius with a wicked grin as he leaned in for another kiss.

Lacy turned her head so she could snort with laughter. "OK, that doesn't even make sense!"

"Oh, yes, it does," growled Darius, rolling his

tongue down along her neck, coating her bare breasts with his clean saliva like he was marking her. Then he opened his jaws wide and took her pert nipple into his mouth, clamping down his lips and sucking so hard she wailed in pleasure. "Close your eyes and think about it while I do some investigating," he gasped just before moving over to give her other nipple some attention.

Lacy moaned as she felt her nipples harden into points as Darius sucked and licked every inch of her breasts. Then slowly he lifted her boobs and licked the warm, hidden space beneath them, making her squirm as his tongue made its way lower, lower, circling her belly button, coating her smooth tummy with his saliva, going lower until she could feel his breath warm and heavy against her stiff little clit.

"Investigating?" she muttered, trying to look down at him but then giving up when she felt his strong hands hold her thighs and ass pressed firmly to the warm wooden floor of the boxcar. "Investigating what?"

"The source of this intoxicating scent," Darius growled from between her legs. "Ah. Found it. Yummy."

"Ohmygod, you pervert!" Lacy shrieked, leaning her head back and laughing as she felt Darius sniff her like a sick, twisted beast. But then the laughter was gone, because he'd pushed his face right in there, his nose driving through her matted brown curls, his tongue landing on her clit just right, flicking it back and forth as Lacy almost choked in ecstasy.

She came just as Darius opened his mouth wide, his thick warm lips kissing her dark nether folds, his tongue somehow still working her clit into a frenzy as he took deep, heaving breaths like he couldn't get enough of her scent, her feminine, her sex. He was still holding her hips down with his strength, and Lacy thrashed and moaned, bucking her hips into his face as her climax whipped through her like a storm.

But it was a storm that was only just rolling in, she realized as her vision blurred and her pants and gasps grew louder. Because now Darius's tongue was rolling around the wet lips of her sex, coaxing her feminine juices out of her like he wanted to drink her nectar, swallow her down, not just claim her but own her, consume her, make her part of him!

"Oh, God, Darius," she wailed as she felt his tongue coat every part of the secret space between her legs, her soft inner thighs, the entire length of her crease, all the way down and around to her dark rear pucker. She was so wet she couldn't tell if it came from her or him, their juices were so intermingled. All she knew was that she was ready. She needed him inside her. Any part of him. *Every* part of him. "Oh, Darius, please. *Please!*"

As she spoke Darius lifted his face up from between her legs, and through tear-filled eyes Lacy looked down along her shuddering, glistening body. Her eyes rested on his cock, and she almost came again when she saw how erect he was, how thick his shaft was, how massive its head. He was oozing from the tip, and as Lacy watched, a heavy bead of his pre-cum dripped down onto her bare belly, just above her dark triangle, the thick natural lubricant pooling on her skin like a royal seal.

He's marking me, she realized as she felt both the woman and the animal in her accept him, accept their mate. Oh, God, he's marking me. And now he's going to . . .

Then she could no longer think, because Darius reached down and pressed the head of his cock to where his pre-cum had pooled, dragging his heavy erection down towards her slit. Lacy felt her wetness pour out of her like a tap, and she wasn't sure if she was coming again or if she'd never stopped coming. It felt like a continuous orgasm, a steady buzz of ecstasy that had taken over both body and soul, woman and bobcat, human and beast.

"You're so wet, Lacy," he groaned, and Lacy just nodded dumbly as she looked down past her glistening boobs to the naked lion Shifter about to claim her. Every muscle on his body was flexed as he fisted his massive cock and rolled its oozing head around the outer rim of her vagina, slowly opening her up. "So goddamn warm. I want to feel you from the inside. I want to claim you from the inside. All the way inside. Every inch of me inside every inch of you. I'm going to open you up, Lacy. Open you up and fill you."

Lacy choked back a swell of ecstasy as she caught a glimpse of Darius's heavy balls beneath and behind his thick shaft, and an image of him emptying himself into her valley bubbled up in her with such clarity that it felt like second sight, like she was seeing the future, gazing upon eternity, looking forever right in the eye.

And then her mouth hung open as Darius finally placed his cock directly in front of her parted slit and took a long breath. Then he looked at her deeply and lovingly, his golden gaze penetrating her soul as he slowly pushed himself into her.

Lacy felt the bulbous head of her mate's cock enter her vagina and stop. She looked up at him and nodded. Then he nodded back, and with a firm, unflinching thrust he drove into her, breaking her seal, entering her boldly, claiming her from the inside, the first, the last, the only.

The only.

8

Even if it were only this once it would be enough, Darius thought as he drove into her with a gentle power that felt like it carried everything he had. The admission that this was the first time for both of them seemed trivial, almost meaningless, like they'd always known they were waiting for each other even though they couldn't possibly have known. Not unless magic existed. Not unless fate was real. Not unless time was an illusion, with past and future existing at once, both with equal footing in the universe.

"This is real, Lacy," he whispered into her hair as he pressed his weight down on her soft, wonderful body and pushed in so deep that he could feel himself opening up new space inside her. She felt so tight against his thickness that Darius was scared he might hurt her at first. But she opened up for him like a flower opens for the rain, and his lion roared inside him as the man filled his mate, took his woman, claimed his queen. "This is real, and it's forever."

He pumped slowly and carefully into her, closing his eyes and reveling in the feeling of discovering her from the inside, the head of his cock dragging against the upper wall of her vagina as he moved back and forth in time with the chug and rattle of the train. The sun had sunk below the horizon, casting a warm, red glow across the African skies. Shadows were dancing on the red-painted metal walls of their moving bed-chambers, and Darius grunted as he felt his balls begin to tighten in preparation for a release so explosive that he wondered if it would destroy them both, perhaps destroy the world itself.

He kissed her again just as the thought disappeared, leaving nothing but pure, unfiltered ecstasy. And then he was coming, the orgasm coming smoothly and silently like a lion stalking its prey, taking its time with the hunt, getting as close as possible before bursting from the shadows like a streak of gold lightning.

"Holy mother of—" he managed to mutter before his eyes rolled up in his head and his body tensed up so tight he lost the power of speech and sight all at once. His muscular ass clenched, and he roared in delight as he felt his mate sink her claws into his back and tighten her legs around his thighs, her body locking him in as he began to pour his seed into her warm depths.

Lacy screamed into the night as Darius thrust with all his might and then held firm, his neck straining as his balls delivered his thick semen into his mate, his cock flexing inside her with each spurt, filling her so completely that he could feel their combined juices flowing down his shaft, coating his balls, marking them both in their fated bond.

They came together as the train blew its whistle as if signaling to every beast in the jungle that the lion had taken its mate, the king had claimed his queen, that fate had won yet again, as if it was proof that the universe and every event in it was perfectly planned.

Perfectly planned, Darius thought with a grin as he collapsed on top of his mate. He could hear the beasts of the jungle call out in the night as if they could sense the magic of two fated mates coming together, and he heard Lacy sigh as his weight pressed down on her like a security blanket.

"Perfect," he whispered, kissing her smooth cheeks and exhaling against her neck. "My mate in my arms. My cubs in her womb. The jungle all around us. Perfectly planned."

But then the train's whistle sounded again, three times in quick succession, and immediately Darius's eyes flicked open as his lion's senses went on high alert. He could feel Lacy's body tense up beneath him, and he knew her bobcat was sounding the alarm as well.

And as the train suddenly slammed on its brakes, sending up a horrible screeching noise as the metal wheels ground against the hot steel rails of the tracks, Darius remembered something his grandparents had said when they'd been teaching the young lion about fate and the universe, destiny and meant-to-be:

"Yes, the universe always has a plan to take you to your destiny," Grandpa had said. "But the catch is that you'll never know the plan until it's all said and done."

"That is the beauty of the universe," Grandma had whispered, a darkness flashing in her wise old eyes as Darius had looked up in awe. "Perfectly planned, but perfectly unpredictable."

Perfectly unpredictable.

9

All her bobcat's plans went flying out the open door of the train-car as Lacy felt Darius leap off her with a lightness that surprised her. But Lacy was on her feet too, every sense of hers on high alert as the train screeched to a halt in the dark African night, the locked metal wheels sending sparks zipping through the blackness like lightning from below.

Lacy fought back a sudden rush of emotion, an image of her sister coming through to her mind's eye. God, in all of this she'd almost forgotten about her own sister! How was that possible? How was that right?!

The answer came to her in a flash as she looked at Darius standing naked, his back to her as he leaned out the open door of the boxcar. His muscular back was lit up by the dark light of the half-moon, and she gasped when she saw three long clawmarks in his skin, deep and fresh, the blood looking black in the muted moonlight.

Then she felt her bobcat hiss inside her just as she became aware of Darius's seed slowly oozing down the insides of her bare thighs, and along with it came a realization that made her shiver.

"You betrayed me," she muttered to her bobcat, her eyes going wide in panic as the guilt of forgetting about her own sister whipped through her like a snake. "In your rush to bond with your mate, everything else took second place! Animal instinct won out over the responsibilities a human has to her family! That can't be right!"

Right and wrong has nothing to do with it, snarled her bobcat, its defiance both angering Lacy and terrifying her at the same time. She'd been in

control of her animal so long she didn't even remember what it was like to actually have it op-
pose the human in her! *It's just nature. Survival.*
Reproduction. Our sister is making the same choices
as we speak. Out here in the jungle, it's every bitch
for herself. And we are in the jungle now, honey. Lis-
ten. You hear it? You hear them?

Lacy swallowed her anger long enough to listen—not that she could have ignored the sounds
anyway: they were too damned loud.

Sounds of the jungle.

The jungle gone wild.

"What's happening?" Lacy said, striding over
to Darius and standing behind him. She touched
his back, blinking at the long clawmarks she'd left
in his skin when the lion had taken her, claimed
her, filled her. "What in God's name is going on?"

"I don't know," growled Darius, his body stiff
and tight, the hairs on the back of his head standing at attention, his golden mane fluttering in the
breeze. "But we need to Change. And we need to
do it now."

Lacy blinked as the sound rose to a deafening
cacophony that sounded like every animal in the
African jungle was screaming at the top of its
lungs. She could hear the wails of the wildebeest,

the rumble of the rhinoceros, the bellowing of the baboon packs as they swung through the thrashing trees. Every bird was awake, from sparrows to vultures, and Lacy swore she heard the snakes slither and hiss, the rodents scurry and squeak, and even the frogs of the forest ribbitt their way to wherever they were going.

"It's a stampede," Lacy said in disbelief as she tried to look past Darius into the darkness. "Something must have spooked them."

Darius frowned and shook his head, his eyes narrowed as he squinted into the black night. "A herd of cattle can stampede. A pack of baboons can get spooked. But this . . . this is unnatural. Every beast of the jungle losing its shit at the same time? Can't happen. No way, Lacy. We need to get out there and see what's going on. Change now, Lacy. You'll need your cat."

Lacy swallowed hard as that feeling of being betrayed by her animal came bubbling up again. Her head was spinning, and she felt her heart pound as once again the reminder that her sister was missing came rushing back along with splinters of guilt. She could feel her bobcat snarl and claw inside her, like it was trying to get out. But Lacy also felt the human in her clamp down with the force of her will, and her eyes went wide as she felt conflict like she'd never felt before.

"I . . . I don't think I can," she stammered, her heart pounding harder as the anxiety rose. The sounds of the stampede were getting closer, the cries of the animals sounding like a nightmare, a scene straight out of the Book of Hell! Perhaps this was the Apocalypse happening! "Darius, I . . . I can't do it."

Darius turned, his face twisted, his eyes narrowed, head cocked as he looked at her. "What do you mean? Just Change, Lacy! You've done it a million times before! Just relax and let your animal come forth! You'll be ripped to shreds if you don't!"

But Lacy could feel herself clamping down, seizing up, and she wasn't sure if she'd lost control of her animal or her human! All she could do was stare up at Darius, blinking as she shook her head, trying to hold back the tears. She couldn't understand what had happened! She was strong, wasn't she? She'd always been strong! Always been in control! What the hell had just happened?!

The sounds of the stampede had risen to fever pitch, the thundering footsteps of the elephants pounding the earth so hard that the train itself was shaking like a matchbox. The combined howls of every animal under the sun sounded like something unholy, and Lacy staggered back from the open door, gasping as she shook her head. She wasn't scared—that much she knew. And although there had been that moment when she was furious at her animal for letting her forget about her sister, it wasn't that either. All her life she'd been able to control her Changes, call her animal forth at will. Her bobcat had always responded with glee when it was called forth. But not now. There'd been a moment when it had tried to get out, but now she could feel it retreating inside her as the sounds of the stampede drew closer.

"All right," said Darius, nodding once, his jaw set tight, his eyes swirling with the power of his lion. Lacy could already see the beast inside him roaring to get out, and she knew she'd have to rely on her mate right now. "Get back. I'll handle this."

Lacy just nodded dumbly, hating herself as she retreated to the corner of the boxcar. This wasn't her! She wasn't some weak, helpless woman who needed to be protected! She could stand toe-to-toe with any man, any beast, face any challenge, win any battle! She didn't need a man to fight for her! To protect her!

"I . . . I'm sorry!" she mumbled, still shaking her head in disbelief as she felt herself come undone. "I don't know what's wrong with me!"

"It's not you," growled Darius as he turned back to the open door of the boxcar. "It's your animal. I feel it in my lion too. There's some strange power at work here. Something dark. Unbalanced. It's confusing our animals. Spooking them. We're Shifters, so I think it hasn't affected our animals as badly as it has these poor stampeding beasts. But it's messing with our internal balance, pulling our animals away from our human side, trying to split us apart from within." Darius glanced back at her, his eyes blazing as he lowered his voice to a whisper. "But we can't be split apart, Lacy. Not now that we're mated." He sniffed the air, cocking his head and listening to the roar of the stampede. "And the animals aren't heading for us. They're going past the train, deeper into the jungle. Stay here, Lacy. You'll be safe here. I need to see what's happening."

Lacy swallowed hard and nodded. A part of her wanted him to stay, and she could see that he wanted to stay with her too, that his lion wanted to protect its mate. But there was another instinct she could sense in Darius, an instinct that was driving him to understand why the beasts of the jungle seemed to have gone insane suddenly.

He's the King of the Jungle, whispered her bobcat from inside her, its voice sending a feeling of calm confidence through Lacy. *And a King needs to know what's threatening his kingdom. We will be safe here. I almost lost it for a moment, but I'm all right now. The lion was right: It was me, not you. I felt a strange urge to come forth and join in the stampede, run wild with these dumb beasts. But then I pulled back. We are mated, and the lion's seed is in us. The power of our coupling created a bond too strong to be broken by whatever force is doing this. Let the King go into his jungle. He will return to us. He will return to his Queen.*

Lacy nodded as she felt her heartbeat slowly wind down, her breathing starting to relax as she felt herself come back into balance. Suddenly she realized that she could Change now if she wanted. She could call her bobcat forth and run alongside her lion. But now wasn't the time. It was still early in their coupling, and Darius's lion might be distracted by the need to protect her out there in the dark jungle. She could take care of herself for now. The lion needed to take care of his kingdom.

"Go," she said softly, nodding her head and setting her jaw. "I'll be safe here. My cat's back. Go, Darius. See what's happening in your kingdom." She paused and took a long breath. "In *our* kingdom."

And the moment she said those last three words, Darius's face broke into a grin, his eyes shining with admiration, with pride, with . . . with *love*! She nodded again, understanding that she was now his primary concern, but she would never be his *only* concern. And she didn't *want* to be his only concern! They were King and Queen of the jungle! They would never have the luxury of just disappearing into some cave and raising their children without worrying about what was happening outside!

She smiled again at her mate, and then she gasped when he turned his head from her and Changed, his lion bursting forth in a flash of gold light, its mane glorious and full, its massive jaws opening wide to let out a thundering roar as if

to say the King was here and he would take care
of everything.

10

Darius felt his powerful haunches warm up as he tore through the jungle, heading straight for the stampeding animals. He wasn't afraid of elephants or rhinos or anything in between, but as he got close enough to see those beasts, he felt a flash of dread go through him.

"What the hell," he muttered, his gold eyes widening as he saw the crazed look in the eyes of the animals. They looked feral, out of their simple minds, wild and rabid. But they weren't actually *running* wild! If anything, they were running in lockstep, strangely orderly, the hippos and baboons and wildebeest galloping alongside in a way that could never happen naturally. It was eerie. No, it was terrifying!

Darius easily kept pace with them, his lion taking long, graceful strides as he watched the beasts of the jungle run. Soon it occurred to him that the animals weren't running away from something; they were running *towards* something!

"What is it?" he growled aloud to a pack of hyenas even though he knew they couldn't answer, that they didn't have the luxury—or the burden—of a human's reasoning, questioning mind. They were being drawn to something like a magnet pulls metal, and as they got closer, even Darius could feel his lion strain against the power.

The moon was no longer visible, Darius realized. They were deep in the darkest part of the Kenyan jungles, so deep that it was quite possible this was nature untouched by human civilization. Pure nature. Pure wildness.

Pure animal.

Suddenly Darius roared as the darkness threat-

ened to overwhelm his lion, and it took a sur-
prising amount of control from the man in him
to get his animal to stop. He did stop finally, but
those galloping beasts were still going strong,
and Darius squinted into the darkness as he realized that the wild animals were literally *disappearing* in the distance!

Slowly Darius moved forward, feeling the
strange magnetism that was pulling the beasts
of the jungle like a black hole sucks in all matter
and compresses it to a point of infinite density.
Every hair on his mane was standing stiff. He
could feel this force trying to split his animal and
his human, but he wasn't afraid of it. He understood that bonding with his fated mate created an
opposing force that would not let his animal get
pulled into whatever this was. But clearly these
simple animals were no match for it. Whatever
it was.

It is the Darkness, whispered his lion as Darius
crept closer and closer to the edge of what seemed
like a wall of pure black.

"Thanks, genius," muttered Darius. "I can see
that it's dark. Telling me that something dark is
darkness doesn't really shed much light on the
matter."

The Darkness, said his lion again, and Darius swallowed hard when he sensed the mesmerizing effect the wall of black was having on his beast. *Pure animal energy. The source of my energy. The source of every Shifter's animal energy.*

Darius frowned as snippets of things his grandparents had told him flickered through his mind: How if an unmated Shifter died, its human went to the Light and its animal returned to the Darkness.

"But . . . but these animals aren't Shifters," Darius said. "Why are they . . . *how* are they . . . oh, shit! Holy motherfu—"

And now Darius felt something he didn't know was possible for him to feel, and it roiled his insides as his lion dug its claws into the dirt, bared its teeth, and stared up at what was emerging through the wall of pure darkness.

Fear.

He felt it like a knife, and it took a moment for him to even understand the feeling. He was a lion, a Shifter, king of the goddamn jungle! Nothing had *ever* scared him or his lion!

Not until now.

Now until this.

Darius's eyes went wide as he blinked in disbelief at the two glowing orbs that were shining through the Darkness. Shining red like fireballs. At first he thought they were planets or moons, that he was really looking into a black hole somewhere in the cosmos. But then he saw a flash of black . . . black that shone with dark light that made his lion's tail go rigid.

"Murad!" Darius whispered as he slowly took a step back. Only now did he realize that the two red orbs were the eyes of the Black Dragon himself! Massive like red moons, unblinking and unyielding, full of fire, powered by all the strength of the Darkness. "The Black Dragon!"

Darius had to fight the instinct to turn and run, and he dug his claws deeper into the dirt and forced himself to stay put. He could feel the pull of the dark energy, and he stared helplessly as the animals of the jungle hurled themselves into the infinite blackness of Murad, the Darkness of the Black Dragon, a gateway that Darius knew was hell on Earth—or at least the beginning of it!

"What's it doing?" Darius muttered as he watched the animals of the jungle disappear as if the Black Dragon was consuming them. Not eating them like a good, normal dragon, but actually *consuming* them. No crunching bones. No blood. Just *poof*! And then they were gone!

Darius's lion didn't answer, and Darius blinked when he realized that he'd taken a step forward without realizing it! His lion was slowly but surely being drawn to the Darkness, and Darius's jaw hung open in disbelief. In that moment he knew he couldn't fight whatever was happening here. Not alone. Perhaps not even with just his mate. He needed reinforcements.

"Not just reinforcements," he growled as he forced himself to turn away from the mesmerizing red eyes of the Black Dragon. "We need a goddamn miracle."

11
TWO DAYS LATER
NAIROBI, KENYA

"Miracle in Morocco!" Lacy said, reading out loud from the newspaper she'd picked out of a trash-can. She raised an eyebrow and looked up at Darius. "Better than the last headline, I guess."

"Chaos in Casablanca?" Darius said with a

snort, adjusting his sunglasses as he slid his arm around Lacy's waist and pulled her close. "I kinda liked that one."

"You just liked the picture of you in that article," Lacy said, feeling a shiver go through her as her mate's arm easily circled her admittedly large belly. "Talk about hamming it up for the camera."

"Hey, I'm a performer, remember?" Darius said as he led her into a crowded marketplace, where street vendors were competing for attention as they hawked their wares. "What are we eating for lunch?"

Lacy squinted up at the blazing overhead sun and then scanned the options around them. The market was bursting at the seams with vendors selling everything from fresh vegetables to dried meat, but although Lacy's bobcat was a carnivore through and through, she couldn't stand the thought of meat right then. Not after what they'd seen in the jungle. Not after what Darius had told her what *he'd* seen.

"Ice cream!" Lacy said, clapping her hands as she saw a group of smiling African teenagers walk by with rapidly melting ice-cream cones in their hands. "Come on!"

"I'm a lion," Darius grumbled, digging his fingers into her side and making her squirm. "I am not eating a goddamn ice-cream cone!"

"Well, too bad," Lacy said, pulling away from him and making her way to the ice-cream vendor. "But since I'm paying, I get to choose. Ice cream. Ice cream. Ice cream!"

"You know," said Darius, finally breaking a smile as he adjusted his sunglasses and pulled his hat farther down his forehead. "I could just say to hell with this disguise nonsense and just show everyone that I'm the Lion Shifter from the headlines. I guarantee I won't need any money to get a taste of whatever that meat-vendor over there is selling."

Lacy sniffed the air and shrugged. "Smells like bush meat. Probably raccoon. The King of the Jungle eating raccoon jerky? My, how the mighty have fallen!"

She felt Darius sigh as they stopped near the ice-cream vendor. The hat and sunglasses wasn't much of a disguise, but no one seemed to recognize them. It probably helped that most of the photographs out there were of the two of them in animal form. And Nairobi was a fairly international city, with tourists, businessfolk, and students from all over the world. They didn't look particularly out of place.

"All right," Darius grunted, letting out another sigh but also giving her side a hard squeeze as if to let her know that this would be remembered when they were alone. "Three scoops for me. Vanilla."

"Vanilla? How lame," Lacy said, giggling as she pulled out her cash. She'd found an international branch of her bank in downtown Nairobi, and since she was a premier client back in the US, they agreed to verify her identity by photograph after she called her relationship manager back in Denver and explained that she was stranded in Kenya without cash or papers.

Of course, she didn't mention that she had no clothes either, because by then she'd stolen some, her bobcat's stealth coming in handy as she sniffed around and found an apartment where the residents were away, snuck in through the window, and found some billowy blue pajamas and a white silk tunic for herself and an Arabesque robe for Darius, who was too big to fit into any of the trousers in the apartment. She'd made a note to return the clothes after buying some new ones, but then she'd decided to just leave some cash instead. A nice surprise, if a bit creepy.

Lacy smiled as she watched her lion Shifter mate instruct the ice-cream vendor to pile on scoop after scoop until the man's eyes went wide. Finally the vendor shook his head.

"Too many scoops," he said in broken, deeply accented English. "It will fall over. Unstable."

"Just keep going until I say stop," Darius growled, his eyes narrowing, the gold swirling in there like liquid. Lacy frowned when she saw the spark of anger in her mate. Then she sighed when she saw him blink and gain control of himself. She didn't say anything. She understood that they were both on edge.

So weird, she thought as they finally strolled away with their ice-cream cones. We've just been hanging out for the past two days, roaming the streets like tourists. It's like we don't even want to talk about what happened that night on the train, what we saw and heard, what we know is coming.

Lacy stopped at a weathered wooden bench near a small city park, gesturing to Darius that she wanted to sit. Darius was pre-occupied with his leaning tower of ice-cream, and he just grunted and stopped, placing one foot on the bench and furiously licking his treat before it melted all over his big hand.

"Miracle in Morocco," Lacy said again, pulling out that rolled-up newspaper and glancing at the headlines. "You know, this is the first article that actually presented all of this in a positive light. I wonder who wrote it." She squinted to read the fine print. "Asheline Brown. Reprinted with permission from the Associated Press."

Darius stopped, raising his head and staring at her. He looked ridiculous, his mouth covered in white ice-cream. But his expression was serious as all hell. "Ash Brown?" he said. "Let me see that!"

"You know her?" Lacy demanded, not sure if she felt jealousy or excitement when she saw her mate toss his ice-cream and feverishly read through the article that he'd previously ignored.

"No. Not really," Darius muttered, looking up and blinking. "It might just be a coincidence. Asheline Brown is probably a common name."

Lacy frowned. "Not really. But regardless, who's the Asheline Brown that you know?"

"I told you—I don't know her. But if I remember right from overhearing Caleb the Wolf and Bart the Bear, Adam Drake's wife is an Ash Brown."

"Adam Drake? The dragon Shifter? The dragon who destroyed that coffee-shop in Milwaukee a few years ago? The one who was photographed carrying a woman out of the rubble in his talons? *That* woman is Asheline Brown? The same one who wrote this article saying Shifters are a miracle, something beautiful and not dangerous, something to be accepted and not feared?"

"Maybe," said Darius. "Possibly. Probably."

"*Maybe*?" Lacy snorted. "How could it *not* be? Of course it is! Darius, we have to get in touch with her! She might have some answers about what's going on here!"

"We already have all the answers we need," said Darius, looking down at his fallen ice-cream cone and smacking his lips. "But not all the food we need. I'm still hungry."

"What answers?" Lacy said. "All we have is questions! Neither of us understands what we saw and heard in the jungle that night! You were truly scared when you saw the Black Dragon! You said it yourself!"

"I don't get scared," Darius growled. "And all I saw was a dragon doing what a dragon does: Feed. Destroy. Consume."

"But it wasn't burning anything," Lacy argued.

"If it was, the entire jungle would have been lit up like a Christmas tree. And you said you didn't hear bones being crunched. You didn't see or smell any blood being spilled. It wasn't *eating* those animals. There was something else happening. Something darker."

Darius shrugged as he grabbed her hand and led her back towards the market, sniffing the air as he made his way towards the meat vendors. "Neither of us has seen a dragon feed. Maybe the Black Dragon was so hungry it was literally inhaling those animals, swallowing them whole. I could do that right now, you know."

"Why are you changing your story two days after the fact?" Lacy demanded, almost stumbling as Darius pulled her through the crowd. She could sense that Darius had made a decision that this was the answer. She could sense that not only was he denying what he'd told her he saw that night, he was also hiding the full story of what he'd felt.

Darius didn't answer, stopping at a meat vendor and ordering a lamb shank the size of her thigh. He waved off the vendor's offer to wrap it, and the shank was half gone by the time Lacy hurriedly managed to get her money out to pay the astonished man.

"Something about what you saw really got to you, didn't it?" she said as Darius finished his meal and began gnawing on the massive bone as people turned to look. Lacy could hear the whispers and comments from the people around them, and she grabbed his arm and tried to pull him away from the gathering crowd.

"One more," Darius said, tossing the bone away and pointing at another lamb shank that was even bigger than the one he'd just devoured.

"This one is to go," said Lacy hurriedly, stuffing some dollar bills into the man's hand as Darius grabbed the shank right off the hook and sank his teeth into it. She smiled apologetically at the locals, many of whom already had their phones out and were taking photos and videos. "Crazy Americans," she said, twirling her forefinger near her temple in the universal signal for "my man is nuts!"

Finally she managed to get Darius out of the market, pulling him into a deserted alley between two concrete buildings. She watched as he finished his meal and hurled the bone at the side of one of the buildings, wiping his mouth savagely and letting out a deep growl of satisfaction.

"So you're a stress eater," Lacy said after a minute of silence. She crossed her arms beneath her breasts and nodded. "Yup. Total stress eater."

Darius snorted, his eyes narrowing with a flash of real anger. "Don't project your own weaknesses on me."

Lacy jolted in shock at the angry comeback, and then her own natural sharpness rose up in response. "Excuse me?" she snarled, her hands on her hips, fists clenched tight, bobcat hissing inside her. "My *weaknesses*? What the hell do *you* know about my weakness?"

"What the hell do you know about *mine*?" roared Darius, his eyes swirling with liquid gold as Lacy heard the lion in his voice. She could sense that his animal was riled up. So was her bobcat—but there was something different about his lion's anger. Lacy couldn't understand it. But she could feel it. She could hear it. She could smell it.

And it smelled like danger.

"Something happened to you in that jungle," she whispered, backing away from Darius as he squared his broad shoulders and began to take deep, gulping breaths, his massive chest rising and falling like he was expending a huge amount of energy. "Something happened to your animal. I feel it, Darius. I sense it. You're off balance. Off center. We need to—"

But Lacy couldn't finish the sentence, because with a roar Darius was on her, slamming her against the rough concrete of the building so hard she almost passed out. And then he was kissing her like an animal, licking her face like a beast, grinding his swollen cock into her crotch like he'd lost control.

"Darius, wait!" she gasped, struggling helplessly as the lion Shifter grabbed her wrists and pinned her arms up over her head. He was biting and licking her neck, pulling her top down with his teeth, inhaling her scent with those deep, gulping breaths. "Darius, listen to me! You're off balance! We shouldn't—"

No, you SHOULD, hissed her bobcat from inside her as Lacy felt a sudden rush of heat go through her, followed by the telltale release of her feminine wetness as Darius rubbed her mound roughly, his strong fingers pushing up inside her through the thin cloth of her pajamas. *His lion is indeed out of balance. It would have been lost to the Darkness if it were not already mated to us. His bond with you saved him that night when he came face to face with the Black Dragon and the Darkness. If not for our fated bond, his animal would have been taken from him, sucked into the Darkness. He felt the pull of the Darkness on his lion that night. For the first time he felt that it was possible to lose his lion, that there might be a power stronger than the King of the Jungle. The event upset the balance between man and animal, and there is only one thing that can bring it back into order.*

Me, Lacy thought as she felt Darius finally rip her pajamas open down the seams, go down on his knees, and ram his face so hard into her pussy that she howled in shock. His tongue was already deep inside her vagina before she even understood what was happening, and she could hear him slurp and swallow like he was drinking her dry.

Me, Lacy thought again as she spread her thighs and gasped at the sight of Darius's head between her legs, his eyes closed tight, his long tongue driving in and out of her, her wetness coating his nose and lips. I have to give him what he needs right now.

But if the animal in him is out of balance, if there's *too* much lion in him, too much power, she thought as he flipped her around like she was a doll, then will I be able to handle it? Or will he break me in two?!

And just as the fearful thought whipped

through her mind, she felt Darius's right palm come down smack on her buttocks, the slap ringing out like a gunshot as Lacy screamed, her eyes flicking wide open as the impact rocked her body. She gritted her teeth and dug her claws into the concrete as she braced herself, screaming again as Darius spanked her hard on her rump three more times before spreading her asscheeks and jamming his face into her rear crack.

He drove his tongue into her rear hole, reaching his hands around her and parting her slit from the front. A moment later he was furiously thumbing her clit, two fingers from each hand driving in and out of her cunt. Lacy couldn't tell if she was screaming or crying, and when her orgasm rolled in, it was all she could do to not pass out.

"Oh, God, Darius!" she wailed, sobbing in ecstasy at the sheer madness of having four of his fingers inside her vagina, his tongue inside her asshole, his body pushing her against the gray concrete of an empty alleyway in Nairobi, Kenya. Her ass was still stinging from being spanked so hard she knew she'd have marks on her smooth buttcheeks in the morning.

If I even make it to the morning, came the

thought as she felt Darius stand up behind her, his hand slowly circling her throat as she felt him press the massive head of his cock against the mouth of her anus, driving his thick shaft deep into her wet canal with such force she couldn't even scream. Just a choking, gurgling, gasping noise came out of her, and then Darius was pumping into her from behind, his hand slowly tightening around her throat.

"What were you saying about weakness?" he growled in her ear, pulling back and ramming his cock back into her rear with a force that made her flesh quiver. "Does this feel weak to you, Kitten? Say meow for your lion, Kitten. Say it."

"Will that make you feel strong, Great King of the Jungle?" Lacy hissed, feeling her stubbornness and fight rising up even though she knew she was being physically dominated so completely that she couldn't even move unless he allowed it. But the woman inside her wouldn't just bow down and submit. That wasn't who she was. To hell with what Darius *needed* right then! To hell with balance or whatever else her bobcat had been going on about. She couldn't just look up wide-eyed at him like a submissive kitten and meow! She was an animal too. She was powerful too. He wanted to own her, to make her bow to him, to make her submit? Well, she wasn't going to do it. Not without a fight.

Lacy snarled as she tried to turn her head, but Darius just tightened his grip on her throat and slammed his hips against her rear cushion, holding his cock all the way inside her rear canal and flexing in a way that made her open up more than she thought was possible.

"Meow," Darius whispered into her hair. "Say it, Kitten. Meow."

Lacy closed her eyes as she felt the opposing sensations of resistance and arousal roll through her as her bobcat wailed in delight one moment, hissed in anger the next.

"Feeling fear doesn't make you weak," she whispered, closing her eyes as Darius continued to pound her against the wall. "Realizing that an enemy is too powerful to face alone doesn't mean you aren't strong. It just means you can't do it alone. That's life, Darius. Partnership. Collaboration. Trust."

"Trust?" growled Darius, pushing into her and stopping so he could lean close. "I told you to Change when the train stopped. But you didn't, and I was distracted by the need to protect your

delicate little human butt while facing Murad. Together we might have been able to do something."

He started to pump into her again, but she
knew her words had gotten through to him. She
could feel it, and finally Lacy gasped as she felt
Darius's energy slowly change, like he was coming
back into balance after that initial burst of lust
that was wild, manic, almost feral in nature. She
shuddered as he kissed her cheek from behind,
stroked her hair gently, caressed her hips and
sides with his big hands. He was still inside her
from behind, but he was holding steady, as if the
physical connection with her was all he needed
right then. The sensation of his body against hers.

"As much as I appreciate you calling my butt
small and delicate," she said, smiling as she felt
him slobber her with gentle kisses, "I doubt that
even the two of us would have been able to do
anything against the Black Dragon. I felt the pull
on my animal as well, Darius. Maybe my bobcat
would have gotten sucked into the Darkness if
I had Changed and run out into the jungle with
you."

Darius stiffened for a moment, and then he relaxed and grunted. "Is that why your cat didn't
come forth?"

Lacy shrugged, blinking as she remembered
the moment she'd felt betrayed by her animal

for forgetting about its own sister, for putting its own need to bond with its mate ahead of the need to protect family! Yes, that was the harsh reality of how animals lived—the need to mate wins over everything else—but it still pissed off the woman in her.

"Did I hurt you, Kitten?" came Darius's whisper, cutting through her thoughts and bringing her back to the moment. She heard the tremble in his voice, sensed the love in the way he carefully ran his fingers along her throat, felt his concern, his gentleness, his need to protect her coming forth, taking over from that need to possess, to dominate, to own. "I . . . I'm . . ."

She waited for him to finish, but he just trailed off, and Lacy snorted when she realized he was still hard and heavy inside her, erect like a beast. "You've never apologized for anything in your life, have you?" she said, almost laughing when she understood how hard it was for the King of the Jungle to say sorry.

Darius grunted against her from behind. "The way I see it, *you* need to apologize first."

"What? Why?" said Lacy, her mouth opening wide as she laughed.

"For calling me a stress eater. That's body shaming, you know."

"What do *you* know about body shaming?"

Lacy said, turning her head halfway and glancing at him askance. "You're a six-foot tall, muscle-bound, circus freak!"

"Is that an apology?" Darius growled, slowly moving his hips and flexing inside her. "It sounds like more body-shaming to me. And I'm six-five, by the way."

"Well, I'm not very good at apologizing either," Lacy whispered, closing her eyes as she felt Darius slowly pull back and then push himself into her again. He was still holding her against the wall, but now the energy felt balanced. Now she could feel the man's love mixing with the animal's need, and it was sending a heat through her that made it hard to speak.

"So that's settled," Darius said, his voice deep and low as he reached around and squeezed her breasts so hard she moaned. "Nobody's apologizing. Excellent compromise, Fated Mate!"

Lacy managed to laugh even though her heat had risen to where it was making her dizzy. "Compromise? You spank me raw, rip my nice clothes to shreds, push me against a wall and ram your . . . *thing* into my rear like an animal. That doesn't feel like a compromise."

"My *thing*?" Darius said, pinching her nipples so hard she yelped. "Were you raised in a Convent? You can call it what it is, you know. The greatest cock in the world."

Lacy snorted, squeezing her buttcheeks tight around "the greatest cock in the world," smiling as she felt her mate groan in pleasure. "Sure," she said. "Whatever you say, honey."

"You know," drawled Darius after gasping against her neck from the way she was squeezing his shaft with her ass, "the more you insult me, the harder I push."

"Circus freak," Lacy whispered, licking her lips and closing her eyes.

"I prefer King of the Ring," he whispered, pulling back and reaching down between her asscheeks. He fingered her rear hole in the most delightfully filthy way, and she could feel him grinning from ear to ear behind her. "*This* ring, Kitten."

Lacy squealed as Darius smacked her bottom and then pushed his cock back into her, opening that rear ring all the way with his girth as she moaned and laughed at the same time. But then she couldn't laugh anymore, because she could feel her mate begin to pump harder, his heavy balls slapping up against her as they swung back and forth.

"Oh, Darius," she moaned, slamming her palms against the concrete wall and bracing herself as her man held her hips and drove with all his power. "That feels . . . it feels so . . . so . . ."

She gulped and groaned as Darius brought one hand around and pressed his big thumb against her throbbing clit, sending a pulse of ecstasy ripping through her body. She could feel her climax building in the distance, like an avalanche slowly beginning its descent down the mountains to the valley. Darius was breathing hard and heavy behind her, and she could sense that he was close to exploding too. They were moving together in harmony, perfect rhythm, their humans and animals in balance again, their bond strong and secure.

"It feels like . . . what?" Darius growled as he rammed into her and held firm, furiously massaging her clit as he pushed two fingers into her vagina. A moment later he was coming, his release blasting into her rear depths like a jet of pure heat, pure desire, pure power, pure . . . love.

"It feels like . . . like . . . like . . ."

"Like what?" groaned Darius, pushing out another spurt of semen into her rear.

"Meow," whispered Lacy, her lips trembling as she felt her climax break through, that avalanche of an orgasm rolling in to meet the release of its mate. "Meow."

12

"**M**eow," he heard her whisper as he poured his hot seed into her rear. The feeling was exquisite, and Darius leaned his head back and roared as he claimed his mate from behind, the lion bringing his kitten to orgasm with perfect control.

Darius finished inside her with a final, deep thrust that sent shivers through Lacy's magnificent curves, and when he was done he just looked down along her hourglass figure from behind, panting in delight as he took in her beauty. She was perfect. So goddamn perfect. Perfect, and his.

Slowly he pulled out of her, groaning as he saw his thick shaft emerge from between her spread buttocks. He was throbbing, oozing, still hard and wet. Hell, he could probably go again right now, she had him so damned aroused!

Yeah, he could go again. But he could also wait. This release had taken the edge off, calmed his lion down, brought him back into balance.

She brought me back into balance, Darius realized as he gently massaged her ass, frowning when he saw the red finger-marks from the way he'd spanked her. A chill went through him when he remembered how he'd put his hands on her throat, held her wrists tight, slammed her against the rough concrete and pushed himself into her from behind. She'd been scared for a moment, he knew. But she handled it perfectly. She gave him what he needed to bring his animal and human back into balance. She submitted, but without yielding. She truly was his equal. His mate. His goddamn queen!

"What are you thinking?" she asked, turning and leaning against the wall, her pretty round face flush from the frenzy of their climax. "Why are you looking at me like that?"

Darius blinked, not sure if he was ready to tell her what he was thinking. He glanced down at the remnants of their stolen clothes. Then he looked around the empty alley. "I'm thinking you might need to steal some more clothes for us," he said.

Lacy giggled. "Well, I have money now. We could just buy some clothes instead of raiding some poor Kenyan family's wardrobe again."

Darius raised an eyebrow as he glanced down at his mate's naked body. Then he reached out and tweaked her nipple hard.

"Ow!" she yelped. "What the hell was that for?" Then she looked down at herself and giggled again. "Oh, right. We're buck naked. Again. In the middle of a crowded city. That's why I like living in the mountains. It's also why I like not having my clothes ripped to shreds by a circus freak."

"Again with the name calling," Darius said, raising his other eyebrow and firmly placing his thumb and forefinger on her other nipple.

Lacy swatted his hand away and laughed. "So sensitive. Though I do feel bad about calling you a stress eater."

"It's OK," said Darius, running the back of his hand down the center of her body, all the way down to her dark triangle of matted curls. Slowly he rubbed her mound, licking his lips and grinning. "I *do* like to eat when I'm stressed. And now that I think about it, I'm feeling a little restless. Better to nip it in the bud before I have a panic attack."

"Well, prevention is better than the cure," Lacy whispered, backing up against the wall as Darius's cock moved in response to the fresh wetness oozing from her slit. "Oh, shit, Darius. What are you doing to me? You've turned me into a . . ."

Darius was already on his knees by then, the scent of his mate overwhelming his senses. He slowly brought his face close to her mound, breathing deep, reveling in the warm, clean musk of her sex. But before he could get a taste of the woman in her, he felt her tense up and push his head away.

"Darius, wait," she said from above him. "Listen!"

"Listen to what?" Darius grunted. The blood was pounding in his ears, and he couldn't hear shit. But when he saw the seriousness in his mate's expression, he stood up and shook his head to clear it.

And then he heard it.

At first it was just the sound of a dog barking.

No big deal. Nairobi was full of stray dogs and cats. But as his inner lion pricked up its ears and listened harder, Darius realized that it wasn't just one dog. It was a lot of dogs. It was *every* dog!

"What the hell?" Darius said, feeling the hairs on his neck stand up stiff. "Am I hearing right? Is that every dog in the city barking?"

"All together," Lacy whispered. "Like a god-damn choir!"

"Or an army," Darius said grimly as the sound rose to a fever-high pitch. "An army of animals."

Just as he said it, they heard more sounds. The mewling of cats. The chirping of birds. The cack-le of the monkeys that hung out in the city and scavenged for leftovers. Even the damned rats were joining in! It was like every animal in the city had gone wild . . . but in a controlled, coor-dinated way!

"Murad," Darius whispered as he thought back to what he'd seen in the jungle that night. "It's the Black Dragon. He's controlling all the ani-mals again. Like his Shifters did to the lion in the circus. Like what I saw in the jungle that night."

Just then Darius heard the screams and shouts of people, and suddenly he knew that it had start-ed—whatever it was! He walked to the end of the alley and glanced out into the street, and what he saw sent a chill through him.

"Change," he said to Lacy as he stared out at a scene reminiscent of the goddamn Coliseum in Ancient Rome, with animals chasing humans, dogs and cats snarling and biting, scratching and clawing, pets chasing their owners, monkeys dropping down from trees like paratroopers as birds swooped down like fighter planes, their sharp beaks bloodied from pecking at heads and necks.

"*Change!*" Darius roared just as his lion burst forth. From the corner of his eye he saw Lacy's bobcat emerge, and he knew he could trust her, that she would be by his side, that he would *need* her by his side.

She was his queen and he was the king.

And right now the jungle needed its king and queen.

13

Lacy felt her bobcat's energy as she raced after her lion, her paws barely touching the ground as she followed her mate's lead. She'd almost frozen in shock at the sight of what was unfolding in the streets of Nairobi; but the moment she'd responded to Darius's command to Change, it was like she understood what to do.

The lion was the King of the Jungle, and she

was his queen. They weren't just fated to be together; they were fated to be *here* together!

With a roar of delight she leaped into the
fray, joining her king in battle. With her strong
paws she knocked the dogs and cats about like
they were toys, pulling them away from the humans and snarling out warnings. Darius was in
full form as his lion, up on his hind paws as he
knocked screeching monkeys from lamp-posts
and trees, batted down the dive-bombing sparrows and crows, casually sent dogs and cats flying ten feet into the air with a swipe of his powerful tail! Lacy might've laughed at the scene if
it had been in a movie—indeed, these were small
animals that posed no threat to a Shifter lion or
bobcat. But the reality was terrifying, Lacy knew.
These were animals that had coexisted with humans for years! They'd all lived side by side in the
city, forming the basis of an urban ecosystem!

"The Black Dragon is shifting the entire balance," she screamed as the realization hit her just
as she grabbed a howling gibbon in her jaws before it sank its teeth into a screaming man's leg.
"On the largest possible scale! Its Darkness is so
powerful that not only can it upset the balance
between a Shifter's human and its animal, but

it's upsetting the balance between human and animal in general! It's pitting human against animal! Darius, listen! I think I understand what's happening!"

"Can we talk about this later?" roared the lion as an army of rats emerged from an open sewer and promptly sank their tiny teeth into his powerful haunches. "I'm been eaten alive by mice! Do something, Kitten!"

Lacy felt her bobcat snarl in delight as she raced toward her lion, picking off the rats like they were M&Ms, gobbling them up without even thinking about it. She wasn't gonna kill any dogs or cats or monkeys. But you can't stop a cat from killing mice. Circle of life, baby. Girl's gotta eat.

"Now that's what I call stress eating!" growled the lion with a wink.

"If by stress eating you mean it relieves *you* of stress, then yeah," snapped Lacy's bobcat, grinning wide as it let out a feminine burp. "And talk about overreacting! Those rats weren't going to eat you! They barely got a nibble out of your big thighs!"

"There you go with the body shaming again," rumbled Darius, swatting away a pack of rabid

Chihuahuas with his tail as Lacy herded some wailing cats with her paws.

Lacy mewed with laughter as the cats hissed and snarled but stood down to the queen's authority. And when she looked up at Darius again, she saw that he was controlling the larger beasts with his supreme authority as King of the Jungle. Slowly but surely the powerful Shifters were controlling the animals, restoring the natural order in a world literally gone wild.

Slowly the surreal battle wound down, and then Darius and Lacy were standing together on the almost comical battlefield, both of them panting, their jaws hanging open in grins as the energy of their divine animals flowed through their sleek, glistening bodies. Around them the dogs and cats and monkeys were milling about like ashamed children, licking their wounds in submission to their King and Queen. It was over. They'd won, and it had been fun!

Lacy nuzzled up to her lion, licking its big face as he slobbered over her nose and made her sneeze. She felt at peace, in harmony, powerful and beautiful. Hell, she could get used to being Queen of the Jungle!

"Excellent performance, Circus Freak," she whispered. "I loved how you knocked those dangerous sparrows out of the air with your powerful paws."

"That took precision and timing," Darius growled, his gold eyes twinkling with warm delight. "Not to mention supreme control. I could have just killed them all, you know. Like you did with the rats." He sniffed her mouth. "I suggest some breath mints, by the way."

Lacy hissed at him. Then she opened her bobcat's maws and breathed out, making sure her mate got the full effect of the rats she'd swallowed.

Then they were both laughing, their animals nuzzling against one another as a peaceful silence descended upon the city. The humans were barricaded indoors by now, and the streets were eerily empty. It was strange, Lacy thought as she felt her bobcat's preternatural sense for danger being activated by a sudden tension in the air. A new tension.

She glanced up at Darius. The lion was standing still and tall, its mane billowing in the breeze. As she watched, the breeze began to pick up, and with it came the unmistakable scent of animal musk.

Big animals.

The animals of the jungle.

"No," she whispered, alarm bells going off in her head. "Darius, you don't think . . ."

"It's classic battle strategy," Darius muttered. "Send in a weaker force to tire out your enemy and give them a false sense of victory. Then bring in the big guns."

As he said it, Lacy heard the sound of trumpets. Of course, it wasn't trumpets. It was elephants. Hundreds of them. Maybe thousands. Soon she could heard the grunts of male rhinos, the squealing of hippos, the snarl of Africa's leopards, the screeching of the larger, more dangerous monkeys.

"Brace yourself, honey," whispered the lion, standing in front of her as the roar of the incoming madness rose to the level of thunder. "These aren't sparrows and mice. We aren't gonna be able to swat these beasts away." He turned to her, and the look in his eye made Lacy want to cry. "We're going to have to play for keeps."

"You mean . . ." Lacy whispered. "You mean we're going to have to kill them?! Darius, no! We can't! You *know* we can't! We're animals too! It's . . . it's genocide!" She swallowed hard, going closer to Darius, her pitch rising as the sound of the attack drew closer. "Darius, maybe that's exactly what the Black Dragon wants! He *wants* us to fight the animals, to believe that we have no choice but to kill them! But we can't! It's a violation of natural law! We kill for food and to protect our young. But this . . . this is wrong! It's murder!"

"You think I don't know that?" snapped Darius. He turned slowly, his majestic lion's body rigid, head held high as he surveyed the scene. The streets were still deserted, but window shades and shutters were moving as people nervously peeked out. Lacy could see that Darius was listening, and soon she could make out the panicked voices of the locals in the distance. No doubt they were calling the police, the military, animal-control, perhaps even the goddamn mafia! This could turn into a bloodbath if the stampeding animals of the deep jungle came rumbling into the city. "But what choice do we have, Lacy? Yes, we're animals. But we're humans too. We're humans *first*, aren't we?"

Lacy hissed through her bobcat's maws. She understood what her mate was saying. They were being forced to make an impossible choice: Choose between humans and the animals. If the

Black Dragon's intention was to throw conflict at them—at *all* Shifters—by forcing them to choose between humans and animals, it was working. She could already feel her animal's restlessness as the trumpeting of the elephants drew near. Could she actually command her bobcat to kill other animals, innocent beasts that were somehow being controlled by the Darkness? Could Darius's lion be commanded to violate its natural position as King of the Jungle by murdering the very creatures it was supposed to lead?!

"No," she said firmly, padding slowly on all fours towards her lion, her bobcat's eyes focused with all the power of the woman in her. "We can't. We won't. We have to stand down, Darius. If we take the bait, we might destroy ourselves, destroy everything that's good in us. Lose control of our animals. Perhaps even lose our animals completely."

The lion turned his head and looked at his queen, and Lacy saw the anguish in his eyes of melting gold. "I can't stand down," he said softly. "These animals are my responsibility. I feel it. I know it. If they've gone wild, then it's up to me to stop them. And I'll do it alone. Get out of here, Lacy. I can't be worrying about your safety when the battle starts. Find Everett the Tiger Shifter.

Find your sister." He paused and took a breath, nuzzling her bobcat's neck and then sniffing her scent. "Protect my children. Raise them. Love them. Tell them about me." He blinked away what Lacy swore was a big fat lion-tear. "Make sure you describe me as heroic and powerful, OK?"

Lacy just stared as she tried to process everything Darius had just said. His children?! Was she pregnant?! Of course she was! His seed would have taken the very first time they mated! That was fate, wasn't it?

The moment the realization hit, Lacy's bobcat tensed up and mewed, and Lacy sensed that it was withdrawing, retreating, desperate to go into hiding. Now that it knew it was carrying its mate's cubs, nothing else mattered but their safety. Reproduction. Survival. The continuation of the bloodline. Millions of years of instinct were damned hard to fight!

"Melodramatic and macho is a better description, actually," Lacy said, trying to smile even though she felt a lump forming in her throat. "I'm not going anywhere. You know I'm not. I'm standing right here, Darius. Right beside you. Either we both run or neither of us runs. If we die, we die together. You said it to me before. Now I'm saying it to you. If we die, we die together."

Don't be a fool, whispered her bobcat from inside. *The lion is right. We are carrying his seed, and we have to protect it at all costs. The lion wants to protect his seed, and so do I. The right answer is to run. That is fate.*

"That may be *your* idea of fate—to mate, get knocked up, and then protect your cubs at the expense of everything and everyone else," Lacy said firmly to her animal. "But a human's fate is larger than that, more complex than that."

"Why are you still here?" roared the lion as the background noise rose to a deafening pitch, with wailing police sirens, whirring helicopter blades, and perhaps even fighter planes getting added to the chaotic roar of the approaching animal army. "I told you to go! Now *go! Run!*"

But Lacy felt a stubbornness settle into her, and although her animal and her mate both wanted her to run, the woman in her wasn't having any of it.

"Nope," she said with a calm determination. "Fate may have brought us together as mates. But fate also put us in this spot, in this place, in the middle of these events. We were meant to solve this somehow, Darius. Think about it: The King of the Jungle smack in the middle of a situation where the jungle has gone insane?! We can't turn away from this!"

"I agree," growled the King of the Jungle. "Do you see me turning away? Godammit, Lacy, you stubborn little—"

But Darius's words were drowned out by a rush of air from above, and Lacy gasped as a massive shadow fell upon them. She looked up and almost fainted when she saw something she'd never believed even existed: A massive dragon, its wings spread wide as it glided low, its scales shining green and gold in the blazing Kenyan sun, its eyes the size of wrecking balls . . . one eye gold, the other green.

"Need some help, big shot?" came a voice from the dragon. But it wasn't the dragon speaking, and when Lacy looked harder she saw three animals on the dragon's broad back: A bear, a wolf, and a fox!

"Caleb the Wolf!" Darius whispered, his gold eyes going wide with surprise. "Bart the Bear! Adam Drake the Dragon! And is that . . ." He raised his snout and sniffed the air like he was trying to figure out who the fox Shifter was.

"The Witch? Magda the Dark Witch? What the motherfu—"

His words were once again drowned out by the rush of air, and the dragon swooped down low with supreme control, its massive talons reaching out and grabbing the lion and the bobcat and tossing them onto its back.

Lacy hissed in delight as her bobcat landed on all fours and instinctively dug its claws between the dragon's interlaced scales. The lion landed with a thud right beside her, the big cat maintaining perfect balance as the dragon took to the skies again, heading straight for the outskirts of the city, to where the jungle met civilization, to the front-lines of the battle.

14

"**T**his is my battle," growled Darius as the wind screamed past his ears. He narrowed his eyes and looked down, his throat tightening when he saw thousands of the jungle's animals rumbling through forest and underbrush, the elephants leading the way like bulldozers, knocking down trees as the other beasts raged along behind them. "Drop me off here. I'll handle this. Take my mate to safety."

"There isn't going to be a battle," came a woman's whisper from the left, and Darius turned. It was Magda the Dark Witch speaking through her fox. "That's what Murad wants. That's what the Darkness wants. That's *all* the Darkness wants: To split humans and animals. That is its essence, and we cannot fight it by allowing our own animals to violate natural law by killing without reason."

"Without reason? Look at these beasts!" Darius roared, glancing at Caleb the Wolf and then Bart the Bear before gesturing down at the nightmarish scene below them. "They're feral! Wild! Rabid! What do you do with an animal gone mad? You put it down! And that's my responsibility! I'm the King of the Jungle!"

Bart the Bear raised a furry eyebrow and then winked at Caleb the Wolf. "I thought he was a circus freak. When did he turn into the King of the Jungle!"

Darius almost leapt at the bear, teeth bared, claws ready. But then the Dragon turned in the air and Darius had to dig in and hang on or else he'd have to learn the fine art of trapeze really damned quickly.

From the corner of his eye he could see Lacy smirk, like she was actually enjoying this. He growled sulkily at her, but he could feel the warmth building inside him when he took in the sight of his mate, the bobcat by her lion's side, powerful and courageous, a true queen.

He was about to say something to her, but through the scream of the wind he heard Magda's low voice. She was muttering something. It sounded like gibberish, but when Darius looked at the witch, he saw that her fox's eyes were burning bright red. Magic! Was she going to control a thousand wild beasts with some spell?! Hah!

"It's not working," Magda muttered, her eyes darting towards Darius for a moment like she'd read his mind, felt his skepticism, his lack of faith in her power. "I'm not strong enough yet."

"Well, I am," Darius growled, crouching down as he wondered if he'd survive the jump from this height. He could land on those trees and break his fall. Perhaps land on one of the elephants.

But the moment he thought of sinking his claws into one of those elephants, a feeling of sickness washed through him like a wave of pure darkness. And in that moment he understood what Lacy had been saying to him, what she'd already understood before his macho ass figured it out:

He couldn't kill those animals.

He had to find another way.

And he couldn't do it alone.

"Try again," growled Caleb the Wolf Shifter. The Wolf glanced over toward the horizon, and Darius followed his gaze until he saw what Caleb was staring at: Attack choppers flying in low over the jungle, cannons set to fire upon the animals before they reached the city.

"I . . . I don't know if there's enough time," Magda stammered, once again narrowing her eyes at Darius as if *he* was the reason her spell wasn't working!

"I'll give you time," came a deep, rumbling voice from beneath them. It was Adam the Dragon, and Darius blinked as he felt the heat of dragon-fire rip through the dragon, almost setting his paws on fire!

A streak of white-hot flame shot out of the dragon's open maws, and Darius stared as he watched Adam set fire to a line of trees a few hundred feet ahead of the stampeding animals. At first Darius wasn't sure if the animals would even stop, they seemed so out of control. But dragonfire wasn't something to be trifled with, and he slowly exhaled as he watched the herd of animals pull up and begin to turn away from the line of fire.

"They're just going to go around the fire," Darius declared, again feeling Magda's gaze upon him.

But Adam the Dragon shook his massive head. Then slowly he tilted in the air, making a giant turn, the precise jet of dragonfire still pouring from his maws. Darius heard Lacy gasp in delight as the dragon circled the animals from above, creating a ring of burning trees that surrounded the animals.

"All you did was start a forest fire," Darius said stubbornly, not sure why he was being so perversely negative. "You're going to burn them all. Nice job, Dragonbreath."

"Darius!" Lacy snapped, her bobcat's eyes narrowing with surprise and then widening as she glared at him. "What's wrong with you? Show a little faith!"

"Faith in what? The Dark Witch who started all this?" Darius growled. "Yeah, bet you didn't know that. This fox Shifter is the reason the Black Dragon has been unleashed on the world! All of this is her damned fault!"

"Faith in your crew," whispered the dragon, turning its head just enough to point its green eye at Darius. "Faith in your mate. Faith in your fate."

"What the hell is he talking about?" Darius

growled, looking at Caleb, the Shifter who'd re-
cruited him to Murad's army. "Is he under some
dark spell that makes him spout nonsense along
with dragonfire? How about you, Wolf?"

But Caleb didn't answer. His eyes were closed
and he was standing close to the fox Shifter.
Darius frowned when he realized that they were
mates, that the wolf and the fox were fated mates!
As he watched, the dark witch closed her eyes and
whispered her spell again, moving closer to her
mate like she was drawing strength from him.

"It's working," Lacy whispered, peering down
and gesturing with her head. "Look, Darius. The
animals are calming down!"

Darius looked down, and although the animals had by no means stopped, their cries and
howls sounded less wild, less out of control, more
like animals and less like goddamn demons. He
glanced over at Magda and Caleb standing close
together. Then he looked at his own mate, feeling an urge to move closer to her.

"They're still gonna burn," he growled, that
weird resistance rising up in him again as he
watched the ring of fire slowly creep inwards towards the animals.

"I told you to have some faith in your crew, in

the team," rumbled the dragon. It turned its head once more, its big green eye winking at the Shifters on its back. "Now hang on."

Darius felt the wind blow back his ears as the dragon descended into a steep dive, its powerful hind legs extended like an eagle about to snatch its prey. At first Darius thought the dragon was going to land, but instead Adam just dragged his talons along the inside of the flaming ring, ripping out trees and underbrush, opening up a wide path between the animals and the fire.

"He's creating a fire-line!" Lacy shouted, grinning at Darius. "Just like firefighters do in California! That way the fire can't spread."

Darius grunted when he realized Lacy was right, and soon he was grinning too when he saw the dragon pull up and create another fire-line on the outside of the flaming ring.

"It looks like a necklace!" Lacy squealed as the dragon rose up again so they could all look down to see the perfectly controlled circle of dragonfire holding the animals in check without burning a single hair on their furry heads! "So beautiful!"

"Not bad," Darius grudgingly admitted. Then he glanced over at the approaching attack-choppers. "But now you've just locked down the targets for those cannons. It'll be like shooting fish in a barrel, Genius."

"Ohmygod, Darius! Are you serious?!" Lacy shouted over at him. "Is your ego so damned big you can't give anyone else credit for doing something useful?! Do you have to do everything yourself?! If you can't save the day on your own, you don't want *anyone* to save the day?!"

Darius was about to shout back at his mate for daring to challenge him in front of the group, but Adam's deep voice drowned them all out.

"The lion is right," said Adam. "Those choppers aren't stopping, and although I could burn them out of the sky, there's no way I'm killing those pilots." The dragon circled in the air once more, then began another dive down towards the trapped animals. "Those choppers' cannons can't do shit to me. The shells will bounce off my scales. Magda's spell seems to have brought the animals back from whatever hold the Darkness had on them—for now, at least." Then the dragon turned his head back, his gold eye focused unblinkingly on Darius. "But now that the animals are back in their senses, they're going to panic at being all bunched up together, surrounded by fire, a dragon blocking out the sun, military choppers creating all that racket. These animals are simple creatures, and their rage is going to be replaced by fear. They're going to need a leader, Darius. They're going to need their king and his queen. I'll provide cover from the attack, but you and your mate need to lead the animals back out into the jungle as the flames die out. They call you King of the Ring, right? Well, here's the ring, King. Now do your thing."

Do your thing, King, whispered his lion as Darius felt an energy that seemed to come from his deepest nature, his very essence. He glanced down at the hordes of animals, and he knew immediately that the dragon was right. The animals were coming out of that strange spell or trance or whatever, coming back to their senses. And their simple senses told them it was time to freak the hell out! They were confused, scared, about to straight-up panic.

He looked over at Lacy, seeing the glint of confidence in her bobcat's eyes as she held her gaze on him. He was still annoyed at her for yelling at him, but he also understood that she was right too: It was hard for Darius to acknowledge that Adam the Dragon was powerful too, could do things that no other Shifter could do.

We all have our place in the world, in the universe's plan, said his lion as it crouched down and prepared to leap off the dragon's back. *And this is our place. In the center of the ring. Let's show them what we can do. Let's do our thing, King. Let's do our thing.*

15

"**U**m . . . so . . . what *is* our thing? What do we do?" Lacy whispered as she landed on all fours by her lion's side, smack in the middle of a cluster of skittish hyenas who were hysterically circling each other, jaws snapping aimlessly as they sniffed the burning wood in the distance, yipped at the sounds of bullets bouncing off the dragon's armored scales above them.

She glanced over at Darius, twin sensations of excitement and anxiety snaking through her as she saw her majestic mate survey the scene with a calm confidence that made her weak in the furry knees. She understood immediately that Darius was in his element now, in the center of the ring, the King surrounded by his subjects. She could feel his power as she watched him, and once again there was that instinctual need to bow down to his authority, to follow his lead. It was pure instinct, and she knew at once that it was an instinct as old as the jungle. It wasn't just a fairy tale: The lion really *was* the King!

"The lion doesn't rule by getting into petty squabbles or fights to prove his strength," grunted Darius as he raised an eyebrow at a panicked hyena that got too close. That one look stopped the beast in its tracks, its snarl turning to a meek whimper as it bowed its head and retreated in submission. "Haven't you ever watched *Animal Planet*?"

"Um, I think this is more like *When Animals Attack*," Lacy muttered, hissing at a group of wildebeest that were snorting and stomping, their tails whipping about even though there were no flies to swat.

"Relax," said Darius with a chuckle.

"*Relax*?! Darius, we're surrounded by a thousand panicked animals! There's a dragon gliding above us, deflecting bullets being shot by the Kenyan military! This is hardly the time to freakin' *relax*! Darius? What the hell are you doing? *Darius*?!"

"It's *exactly* the time to relax," said Darius, his voice calm and steady as he plonked himself down on a patch of grass. "Come. Sit by me."

Lacy whirled around in confusion, not sure if her mate had lost his mind. But then she saw how a group of monkeys that had been sounding the alarm in a nearby tree had stopped thrashing about and were now all staring at the lion . . .

The lion who, in the midst of confusion and chaos, was just chilling the hell out.

Then Lacy understood. She got it. She got *him*!

With a slow, deliberate walk, Lacy padded over to her mate. She leaned in and nuzzled against his big furry neck. Then she sat by his side, her bobcat's body nestled perfectly against the lion's massive frame. She could feel the protective energy oozing from her mate as he calmly looked at all the animals of his realm, and she understood exactly what he was doing.

"I get it now," she whispered, her eyes lighting up as she saw how all the animals were instinctively calming down in reaction to seeing the lion and his mate sitting down like they didn't have a care in the world. "You're leading by example. You're showing them that there's nothing to worry about, that it's all gonna work out just fine, that the King and Queen say it's all right. Just chillax, people!"

Darius just grunted, his big gold eyes gleaming at her in acknowledgement that she was right, that she understood how instinct worked, how the lion and his mate set the tone for the rest of the animals. The jungle was at its calmest when the lions were well-fed and relaxed, and this was exactly what they needed to do in the midst of the madness. Just relax.

And then Lacy felt a strange peace roll through the atmosphere, and soon she and Darius were rolling around, playfully biting at each other as they lost themselves in the magic of the moment. In the background Lacy could sense that the flames were slowly dying down, the ring opening up a pathway back to the jungle. The barrage of bullets above them seemed to have lessened too, and Lacy finally rolled onto her back and glanced up at the massive dragon flying cover over the king and his queen.

"Darius, look," she whispered, pointing with her right paw. "The choppers are leaving. Either they're out of ammunition or they've figured out that it's pointless to pepper a mythical beast with silly little bullets!"

Darius grunted, barely even looking up as he rolled belly-up and scratched his back on the hard ground. "What about the animals? Are they heading back to the jungle?"

Lacy rolled onto her side and looked around. "Yes," she said as she watched the animals slowly leave the area through a path cleared by the elephants. The fire had mostly died down, leaving smoldering wood and scorched earth that smelled like incense.

"Then it's time for us to go," Darius said, getting to his feet and glancing up. He waved at the dragon like he was hailing a taxi, and Lacy gasped as the winged beast circled once more and then came in for a landing. "The animals are safe, but we aren't."

"What do you mean?" Lacy asked as she bounded up onto the dragon's back, nodding at the bear, wolf, and fox that had been hiding behind the dragon's massive dorsal wing. "You think the Kenyan military is going to send in fighter jets next?"

"They already did," Adam the dragon said, pushing off against the earth and taking off into the skies with ease, five Shifters on his scaly back. "They launched a few missiles, but then stopped when they realized I wasn't fighting back. Either that, or they were called off. Ordered to stand down."

"Who would have called off the attack?" Darius growled, raising a gold eyebrow. "And why? As far as the world knows, Shifters are dangerous, out-of-control monsters! They probably think that *all* those animals were Shifters running wild! Shifters are primetime news now—and *bad* news! Who the hell would have called off the attack?"

Bart the Bear and Caleb the Wolf both shot one another knowing looks before breaking into chuckles. Beneath them Adam the Dragon was rumbling with laughter too, and even the Dark Witch Magda cracked a smile through her fox.

"You ever heard of John Benson?" Caleb the Wolf said finally as the dragon set course and picked up speed, heading directly Northeast from Africa, towards the Arabian Peninsula.

"No," said Darius.

"Exactly," said Bart the Bear, his massive brown body quivering as he giggled like an overgrown schoolboy. "That's just the way he likes it."

16
ABU DHABI
UNITED ARAB EMIRATES

"I don't like it," said John Benson, pulling at his silver beard and frowning so deep Darius could see every crease on the weathered CIA-man's forehead like it was a map of where he'd been, what he'd done, what secrets he kept locked away inside that head. "I don't like it one damned bit!" He turned directly to Darius, gray eyes shining with focus. "You said you saw Murad? The Black Dragon himself? The beast is in Africa? Why didn't he attack you? Why didn't he attack *all* of you? Why didn't my drones and scout-planes pick him up visually or even on radar? Are you sure it was him?"

"I know what I saw," Darius said, his gold eyes flashing as he held Benson's gaze. "But it was strange, I agree. I could sense the dark energy of the Black Dragon—shit, it almost pulled my lion away from me! But there was also a strange sense of control in the beast. It's like it knew what it was doing, even though it didn't know what it was doing."

Bart the Bear stomped his feet and rubbed his eyes. "It knew what it was doing even though it *didn't* know what it was doing? Wow, that really clears it up, Lion King! I'd get a better explanation just banging my head on the wall!"

"Happy to help you with that, Furball," growled Darius, feeling his lion whisper that it would be more than happy to pound this dumb bear into submission on Benson's teakwood tabletop.

Bart grinned wide, sticking out his chest as he turned to face Darius. "You wanna throw down,

Big Boy? Let's go. I'll have you mewing for Mama before you can even—"

Adam narrowed his eyes at Bart, and the big bear Shifter sighed and raised his hands. "All right. All right. I'll save it for later."

"Mama," came Magda's whisper from the left, and Darius frowned as he turned to face the Dark Witch, who'd been quiet all this while. "Mama."

"What the—" Darius started to say, but his breath caught when he saw how Magda's eyes had rolled up in her head, her eyelids quivering, lips trembling. "What's she doing?"

Instinctively Darius stepped in front of Lacy, but she was having none of it. She pushed her way around his thick body, going straight to the convulsing witch and grabbing her by the arm.

"What is it?" Lacy whispered, her eyes wide and earnest. "What do you see?"

"She's having a seizure, Lacy," Darius growled. "Step back. She might bite you."

"She's having a vision," said Lacy firmly. "Can you just show some faith for once?"

"She's a goddamn witch," Darius snapped. "You don't show faith in a witch. That never ends well. She started all this, and for all we know, she's still working for Murad. Hell, maybe Murad's working for *her*! Maybe we're *all* just puppets in her twisted game!"

Now Caleb the Wolf stepped forward, his blue eyes the color of midnight, his wolf coiled up like a spring inside. Bart the Bear stepped up and stood by his buddy's side, and Darius could sense a fight coming on. He let out a low, warning growl from his lion, shooting a quick glance at Adam Drake. The dragon was the only Shifter more powerful than a lion, but Darius could sense that Adam wouldn't Change in this enclosed space in the middle of freakin' Abu Dhabi! Not unless he wanted to kill all of them!

The tension was so thick Darius could almost see it. From the corner of his eye he saw John Benson slowly back away from the desk, like he knew he'd be ripped to shreds if three Shifters got into a rumble in his office. As for Magda . . . well, Darius didn't trust Magda. He didn't trust witches. He didn't trust . . . Mama?

Darius blinked in confusion as memories of his childhood came rushing in like a dam had just broken. He cocked his head as he stared at Magda, wondering if she was doing something to him, messing with his head. He'd buried the memories of his parents—buried them because he *had* no real memories of them. He'd been alone after his grandparents had died too—surviving on his own in the woods, learning to hunt, learning to kill, learning that he couldn't rely on anyone but himself, couldn't trust anyone but himself.

For some reason Darius kept staring at Adam Drake as the thoughts rushed in, and as the dragon Shifter stared back, Darius felt a strange bond form almost instantaneously between the two of them. A kinship of sorts. An acknowledgement that Adam understood what it was like to not trust a parent, to perhaps even hate a parent!

Slowly Darius scanned the tense faces of Bart the Bear and Caleb the Wolf, and in their eyes he could see pain and heartache, a history of abandonment, tragedy, misery. They were all bound together by hardship, he began to realize. Bound together like brothers. Bound together by . . . fate?

The lion inside was slowly retreating from its readiness to fight, and Darius felt the calmness of the man in him slowly win as he looked over at Lacy and then back at the men. She was his fated mate, yes. But what had she told him earlier? She'd said an animal's fate begins and ends with finding its mate, but a human's fate is broader, bigger, more complex.

So these men are part of my fate too, aren't

they? Part of my crew! I'm part of *their* crew!
That's the source of all this machismo and tension! We're sizing each other up, jostling to figure out what our place is in the crew. Adam might
be the Alpha, but we're all leaders, all warriors,
all proud men who never bow down, never submit, never yield! That's a new challenge, isn't it?
To learn how to work with others as powerful as
I am? To respect the unique talents of my crew-
mates? That's what a good king does, right?

"All right," he said finally, exhaling but not taking a step away from Bart and Caleb, holding their
gaze until there was a moment of mutual understanding and they all looked away at the same
time so no one could admit defeat. He let out
a slow smile and looked over at Lacy, his heart
filling with a warmth that felt both peaceful and
wild at the same time. She'd brought him to this
moment, he understood. It was her, whether she
knew it or not.

"All right," he said again, glancing at Magda
and then back at his mate. "But if she bites you,
I'm gonna say *Told You So.*"

Everyone in the room laughed, and just then
Magda gasped and came out of her trance, blink-

ing three times and breaking into a bewildered smile like she was trying to remember where she was.

"I saw his mind," she said, her voice coming out in a whisper. "I saw his heart. I saw what he sees in his madness." Slowly she turned to Adam, her eyes glistening with tears. "He sees you, Adam. His child. He sees you as a baby. A baby dragon crying for Mama. And he's crying for her too."

"Crying for her? He *killed* her!" Adam said, his eyes burning in a way that made Darius tense up, wondering if the dragon was going to burst forth and destroy the building!

"That's what he thinks too," said Magda, her eyes widening as she glanced at her mate Caleb and then at Adam. "Even his dragon thinks its mate is dead. But she isn't. Adam, your father didn't attack her in some rampage. He did it because . . . because he was trying to *Turn* her!"

"That's ridiculous!" Adam shouted, clenching his fists as smoke billowed out of his nostrils and ears. "A dragon can't Turn a human! He would have known that! He would have known he'd kill her! His dragon would have known it too!"

Magda shook her head. Then she shrugged.

"Well, whatever it did to her *didn't* kill her, and your father is only just realizing it. The Black Dragon is only just realizing it."

Adam was pacing, rubbing his jaw as Darius watched, his lion growling inside, ready to protect its mate in case things got out of hand.

"So wait, that's a *good* thing, right?" said Lacy excitedly. "Doesn't it mean the Black Dragon might not be lost to the Darkness? That there's hope it will find its way back from feral madness?"

But Magda shook her head slowly, her eyes darkening in a way that sent a chill through Darius. "The problem is that Adam is right: A dragon can't Turn a human without killing the human. And that *is* what happened—sort of." She paused and blinked, shaking her head again. "Adam, when your father's dragon attacked your mother to Turn her, it worked almost *too* completely! It killed her *and* it Turned her!"

"What the hell does that mean?" Adam roared, pacing around the room as if his dragon was fighting to get out.

"When s Shifter dies, the human goes to the Light, and the animal returns to the Darkness," Darius muttered, thinking back to what his grandparents had told him as he tried to make sense of

Magda's vision. "But what happens if a non-Shifter is Turned *and* dies at the same time?! Is that what you're saying happened, Magda? That Murad's Black Dragon killed his mate and Turned her at the same time?! Creating some kind of dragon that has no human part?"

Magda blinked and nodded, for the first time looking at Darius without frowning. "Yes," she said softly, sighing and then glancing over at Adam. "It shouldn't have worked, but it did."

"So the human in her returned to the Light, but there was a new Dragon forming too . . . and that new Dragon has spent its entire existence in the Darkness," Darius said as the awful realization began to dawn. "A Dragon *born* from Darkness! A beast that has *never* been joined with its human!"

"So where is she? Adam's mother? Murad's mate? This other dragon?" Lacy said, frowning as she glanced around the room at the ashen faces of the group.

"I don't know," Magda whispered. "I think she hasn't emerged into our world yet. But she's coming. I think Murad's Black Dragon has been waiting for centuries for its mate to evolve, to emerge, to return! But the Black Dragon also knows that it will never be able to truly bond with its mate, since she has no human in her at all! It wants its mate, but can't have her! That's frustration, anger, chaos! Which means there might be *two* feral Black Dragons loose on the world soon, both of them driven insane by a bond that can never be complete! I think that's what you saw out there in the African jungle, Darius. A new gateway to the Darkness is opening up for Murad's mate, Adam's mother, to crawl out!"

Bart the Bear stepped forward, his big brown eyes widening as even he began to understand what was happening. "Like the gateway to the Darkness in Germany? The souls of my parents are guarding that doorway. So who's guarding this new one? Who's gonna make sure Adam's crazy mama doesn't bust out and destroy the world?!"

"My mother is *dead*!" rasped Adam. "Whatever my father created in his attempt to Turn her is *not* my mother! It's a goddamn demon!" He stopped pacing, his jaw tightening in determination, his gold left eye burning so bright Darius had to blink. "And so is my father, as far as I'm concerned. This has gone on long enough. We know where he is, right? We know where that new gateway to the Darkness is, right? All right then! Enough talk. I'll finish this once and for all. I'll kill them both. I'll do it. I'll kill them both."

"No way, Adam!" Caleb the Wolf said, his blue eyes widening as he shook his head furiously and then turned to his mate Magda. "There has to be another way. Magda, you have to be able to do something with your magic! Bart's parents said that you were the key, didn't they? That you'll find a way to combine both Dark Magic and Light Magic to . . . to stop what's happening!"

But Magda just blinked, her round face looking so white Darius thought she might faint. He could already sense Adam's dragon coming close to the boil, and when he looked over at the tall Dragon Shifter, he saw the man staring at the big window as if preparing to jump from the building and Change. Adam was the Alpha of the crew, yes. But even the Alpha could be wrong sometimes. Even the Alpha needed help. Even the Alpha sometimes needed a member of his crew to step up and take the lead.

Time seemed to slow down for Darius, and he felt his lion surge inside him. But it wasn't yearning to bust out. In fact it was a surge of confidence, the same kind of energy that had quieted down those crazed animals back in Kenya. Slowly he surveyed the room, sizing up every participant in the game that was unfolding: Caleb and his witch. Adam close to losing control and heading off to kill his own parents. Bart the Bear taking short, quick breaths as his animal thrashed inside him.

"Hey, Bear," he said to Bart as he suddenly understood what needed to be done. He lowered his voice to a whisper, gesturing with his head towards the fuming Adam. "Can you hold Adam in check? Can you hold his dragon back?"

Bart blinked, a wide grin breaking on his face as if he was delighted at being given a clear mission that needed brute strength. "That I can do, Lion," he growled, and a moment later his bear burst forth, sending chairs flying across the room as the massive beast leapt at his Alpha, trapping him in a bear-hug so powerful it would have killed any normal man.

"Bart!" roared Adam as sparks flew out of his mouth and nose. "I warned you that if you ever tried this again, I'd . . . Bart! *Bart!*"

Darius blinked and took a step back as he saw Adam's dragon trying to burst out, but the Bear Shifter was somehow holding it inside with pure strength. After several minutes of shouting and grunting, Adam finally went limp in the bear's hug, shaking his head and sighing as his rage subsided.

"Good," said Darius, his jaw tight as he turned to Caleb and Magda. "Now what's this about magic and spells? Are you saying there's a spell that can close up that new gateway? Or tame two feral Black Dragons?"

But Caleb was holding his mate close, trying to comfort the distraught witch, who was simply shaking her head like she didn't know what to do.

"I'm not powerful enough yet," whispered Magda in despair. "And I don't know what I need to do for that kind of power!"

"I do," came John Benson's voice from the corner of the room, and everyone turned to look at him. "That power will come from those around you. It's not just your power—it's *everyone's* power. Your entire crew's combined power." He slowly stepped forward, now that it was clear Adam's dragon wasn't going to burst out and destroy everyone in the room. "Take a look at yourselves, guys! Look at how you all have been drawn together by fate, by the universe, by your individual and combined destinies! Each time you added someone to the crew, Magda's magic grew more powerful, didn't it?"

Darius frowned as every Shifter in the room looked at one another. "So if she's not powerful enough yet, then it means we're still missing someone."

"Well, yeah! My sister!" Lacy said, her eyes wide as she turned to Darius.

"And her mate Everett," he whispered. "The Tiger. We have to find them."

"Well, *that* I can help with," said Magda, finally letting out a smile. She stepped forward and nodded at Lacy. "Hold out your arm. There we go."

"Ow!" Lacy said, staring down as Magda ran her sharp fingernail along her bare arm, drawing blood. "What the hell?"

"Hey!" roared Darius, leaping forward, about to grab the witch and pull her away.

"It's OK!" Lacy said hurriedly, raising her hands to stop him. "I'm OK! Let her do her thing, Darius. It's OK."

Darius growled as he forced his lion to simmer down. Then he nodded, and Magda slowly clenched her fist, Lacy's blood staining her tight fingers. She muttered a few words under her breath, and then her eyes rolled up in her head as she swayed back and forth like she was going into a trance.

"Well?" said Lacy anxiously. "Where are they?"

"Honeymoon suite in the Bahamas, probably," said Darius, trying to break the tension as they waited for Magda's reply.

But the tension only rose, and when Magda opened her eyes again, they were blood red. "I . . . I can't see her. I guess my spell didn't work. Sorry." She turned to her mate. "Caleb, we should go. I need to rest. Regain my strength." She glanced apologetically at Lacy, but Darius could tell she was holding something back.

"Liar," he growled, feeling the distrust rising up again. He reminded himself that this was still a Dark Witch, a woman who'd orchestrated Murad's rise, controlled the Black Dragon who was poised to raise hell on Earth. He glanced at Caleb, holding the Wolf Shifter's blue-eyed gaze until the Navy Seal finally took a breath and nodded as if he agreed with Darius's accusation.

"What is it, Magda?" said Caleb softly. "You need to tell us."

But Magda shook her head violently, pleading

with her eyes. "I can't be sure. And I can't say it unless I'm sure. I need some time to—"

"She's dead," came Lacy's voice, and Darius whipped his head toward her when he heard the chillingly confident tone. "My sister's dead, isn't she?"

Every set of eyes turned to the Dark Witch, and finally she lowered her blood-red gaze and nodded.

"Yes," she said. "I'm sorry."

"Don't be sorry," said Lacy, looking up with a grim smile on her pretty round face, tears rolling down her cheeks. "It's not your fault. It's mine." Then she turned to Darius, those eyes of hers looking right through him, her gaze cutting like a knife. "And his, for convincing me Tracy would be safe with the Tiger!"

"Mine?" said Darius, frowning and taking a step forward. "What the hell are you talking about, Lacy? Look, we don't even know if she's dead. Hell, she *can't* be dead! Everett the Tiger would have protected her with his life!"

"He did protect her with his life," came Magda's trembling voice. "Or at least he tried."

Darius felt dizzy as he turned to look at Magda, then whipped back around to his mate. Everett was dead too? No way! The guy was one of the most powerful Shifters he'd ever seen! And he was smart as hell too! How the hell could—

But his thoughts were washed away by a sudden movement. It was Lacy, moving with the quickness of her bobcat! She'd leapt towards Benson's desk, knocking him aside and yanking open the top drawer. A moment later she pulled out a shiny black handgun and held it against the side of her head as everyone in the room gasped.

Darius roared as he prepared to Change and leap at his mate. But she stopped him with a simple look, a look that almost brought the Lion to his knees as he felt his world threaten to shatter around him.

"Lacy," he managed to mutter through his rapidly tightening throat. "Are you insane? What are you doing? If you pull that trigger while in human form, you'll . . . Lacy, give me the gun. Give me the fucking gun!"

"She's my twin, Darius," Lacy whispered. "She's a part of me. I have to go to her."

"I said give me the gun," Darius commanded, gritting his teeth so hard he could feel them wearing down.

"I . . . I . . ." Lacy stammered, and Darius could

see the conflict in her eyes. He understood that she'd followed her animal's primal need to bond with its mate when the two of them had met. But now that they were mated, the human in her was being destroyed by the guilt of not searching for her sister earlier.

Now that they were mated . . . came the thought again as Darius frowned. A chill passed through his tense body as an idea so wild, so dangerous, so insane emerged that he almost choked.

Mated Shifters never die, his grandparents had told him. *They stay mated forever. If an unmated Shifter dies, its human and animal split—the human going to the Light, the animal returning to the Darkness.*

"So where does a mated Shifter go if its body is destroyed?" Darius wondered out loud as he stared at his mate holding the gun to her head, a look in her eye that seemed to match the crazy idea that was forming in his own mind.

A mated Shifter can travel between Light and Darkness, came the answer from his lion. *That is the power of the fated bond. She wants to go after her sister, bring her back, put her together again. And you need to go with her. Trust that the witch will find a way to bring you both back.*

But she's pregnant, Darius thought as panic

rose up once again. If she pulls that trigger, what happens to our unborn cubs?!

If the witch brings you two back before the pregnancy reaches term, our cubs will be unaffected, replied his lion. *Her bobcat understands that too.*

And her animal is willing to take the risk? Gamble with the lives of its cubs? I don't believe that! Darius shot back at his lion. And you're willing to take that risk too? I thought the animal's only instinct was to preserve its young!

Well, your animal has been cursed with the wisdom of the human, grumbled his lion. *Both the bobcat and I understand that if we can't stop the Black Dragon before its dark mate emerges, then we are all doomed—cubs, kittens, pups, and everything in between. There comes a point when the King and Queen must put it all on the line to save the universe. That's our responsibility and ours alone. Yours and hers. Get it, King of the Ring? She gets it. Now show some faith in the members of your court. Show some faith in your crew. Show some faith in your mate. Show some faith in your eternal bond. Make a decision, King. Pull the trigger.*

Slowly Darius nodded as he held his mate's gaze. Were his grandparents right? If they pulled the trigger, would he and his mate be able to traverse both Light and Darkness with the power of their bond? Would they be able to find Everett and Tracy? Did Everett and Tracy complete their bond before dying? How did they even die in the first place?! Would the witch's magic be able to bring them all back in time to save his unborn cubs . . . not to mention the entire goddamn world?!

Only one way to find out, he thought as he remembered that a Shifter's destiny was bigger than just finding its mate, that he had to follow his path no matter where it took him.

He had to follow his path, and his mate. Their shared destiny. There was no standing down. No turning away. The King and Queen didn't have that luxury.

"We each said it once to the other: That we'd die together," he said softly, his unblinking gaze focused on Lacy's determined eyes as he slowly walked to her. Darius placed his head in line with hers, their cheeks touching as he reached for her trigger finger. Slowly he began to squeeze her finger as he breathed deep of her scent. "So all right, you crazy kitten. If this is destiny, I'll be right there with you. Right there with you, babe. All the way to the end. In Darkness and in Light.

In this life and whatever lies beyond. Always and forever, Kitten."

Always and forever.

∞

FROM THE AUTHOR

OMG, listen: Those of you who've been reading me for years know that I never do cliffhangers like this, but Lacy and Tracy's stories are too in-tertwined to separate fully (they are twins, after all!). This book had to end here, because we need to see Tracy and Everett's bonding to truly finish the story.

Maybe you hate me now, but I beg of you to have some faith! TAKEN FOR THE TIGER is the last book in this series, and we'll get the final Happy Ending we all crave!

And yes, I crave it too! I'm along for the ride just like you guys are! This isn't some trickery just to get you to buy another book! Those who know my work understand that I always stay true to my muse, even if it pisses off my readers (Haunted for the Sheikh, anyone . . . ;))! I could have just put in another sex scene and an epilogue showing Lacy and Darius and their cubs, but it wouldn't have been true to the way the story is playing out.

Thanks for coming this far.
I do hope you stick with us to the end.

Love,
Anna.

PS: In the meantime, do consider my long series of standalones, CURVES FOR SHEIKHS. And I've got a new super-hot Curvy-girl series of stand-alones dropping in July! OMG, please don't hate me!

Made in the USA
Las Vegas, NV
11 August 2023